The *Loathe* Boat

CINDY DORMINY

The Loathe Boat
Red Adept Publishing, LLC
104 Bugenfield Court
Garner, NC 27529
https://RedAdeptPublishing.com/

---

1. http://StreetlightGraphics.com

Chapter One

Chrissy

Nothing says love like walking through a parking garage in a bright-yellow duck suit. The constant side-eye from fans entering the Nashville Crooners hockey arena makes me jut my chin even higher. I'm rocking this costume, and after I win the contest, all the odd glances will be totally worth it.

As I wedge myself between six people in the elevator headed up to the VIP section, I do my best to keep my confidence high. Even though I'm not embarrassed, my stick-in-the-mud father will definitely toss snide comments my way, but I've learned to ignore them and pretend they don't bother me. When the elevator pings, signaling the club level, I strut—or better yet, waddle—down the corridor toward the Parks and Doyle Wealth Management suite.

I wave my feathered hand at an attendant as I enter the suite. The room is filled with men decked out in business casual attire, some standing in small groups, while others sit at the high tables, sipping drinks as they feast on the buffet items, which are almost too pretty to eat. Several of the younger men have made their way down to the two rows of seating to actually watch the hockey match. My favorite part of this suite is the private bathroom—not having to wait in line down the hall to pee is quite lovely.

In the middle of the room stands my father, drink in hand, and I let out an audible groan when I realize he's chatting with Elliot. I shouldn't be surprised that he's here since he is climbing the ladder at my father's financial institution, but the fact that he's my ex-husband tends to make things a tad bit awkward. We're still friends, but the "with benefits" part didn't work for us. That ship sailed, and unlike the cruise I want to win from this contest, I have no desire to get on that boat ever again.

While most people at the arena are decked out in the Crooners' two-tone blue, Dad wears an Armani suit. He's never completely off the clock. He tried wearing a jersey over his suit one time, and he just looked so silly that he decided to stick with what he knows best: high-end business attire. His company motto is "Unlock Your Financial Potential," and he lives it twenty-four seven. *Boring.*

Deciding it's best not to interrupt the conversation Elliot and Dad are having, I backpedal to exit the overcrowded room, but my tail feathers hit a dessert tray, sending mini cheesecakes crashing to the floor. That's a shame because I adore them so much. I could eat a plate full of them.

All eyes pivot toward me, especially Elliot's. His expression changes from surprise to a tiny headshake before he rolls his eyes. He needs to lighten up a bit, and I'm not talking about what I can only assume is his fifth drink of the night already.

Dad's brow scrunches. "PC, what on earth are you wearing?"

Tamping down my irritation from Dad not remembering what I'd just told him yesterday—along with his calling me that silly nickname, which makes me feel like a computer—I allow a fake smile to slide across my face. "I'm in the contest at intermission, remember?"

Elliot points his glass in my direction as he addresses my father. "She and what's his name made it to the final round of the Cruisin' for a Cruise competition."

Realization forms across his face. "Ah, yes. I remember now. The boyfriend."

I blink a few times but catch Elliot's mouth twitching. "Yes. Deacon."

Dad scoffs as though this is the most ridiculous idea ever. "If you wanted to go on a cruise so bad, why didn't you just put it on my card?"

"Where's the fun in that?" I do my best to keep a playful tone in my words, but I refuse to tap into the family funds if I can help it. There is always a price to pay, and it doesn't involve money.

Elliot rolls his eyes because he never had a problem letting my father pay for everything when we were married, even though he came from money too. Although he's the ex, he has been cordial toward Deacon, which is a relief. When I got the nerve to admit I'd never been in love with him, he bowed out of the relationship without making a fuss. Deep down, he knew and might have been a bit relieved. Elliot only wants me to have someone who makes me happy, someone who wants the same things in life as me. And Deacon is absolutely perfect for me.

With one last wave of my feathered hand toward the room of businessmen, I leave the suite, hoping I'm not going to be late for the competition. Strutting right toward me is my adorable boyfriend. He's suited up, and even in a fluffy costume, he makes my heart thump fast in my chest. I never get tired of his sea-green eyes, which sparkle when he grins, and that tousled, just-showered sandy-blond hair. Even though he's completely covered in feathers, he has a rock-solid body. He's one of those guys who practices what he preaches.

"You shouldn't go waddling around by yourself. No telling what kind of quacks will take advantage of a little duckling like you."

I nudge him with my hip. "I wanted to say hello to my dad."

Deacon's jaw flinches. "How is Mr. Parks?"

"Dad's the same. Elliot's here too, hobnobbing, as usual." I let out a sigh.

Deacon knows my struggles with my father, how I like to zig when Dad thinks I should zag. And he especially knows the continuing working relationship Dad has with Elliot. I've done my best to keep nothing from Deacon. It's one of our rules. Failed relationships have taught us both that it never ends well when someone isn't completely truthful.

He shakes his head as he stares down at me. A storm of emotions wafts across his face before he blinks them away. "I still can't believe you married that guy."

"I'd like to think I learn from my mistakes. Besides, he's still a very good family friend."

Deacon harrumphs then releases my shoulders, and we walk in silence for a while. I wish I could read his thoughts, because he must know by now that I have no romantic feelings for Elliot.

He clears his throat, bringing me back to the present. "I hope so, because I think you are about the cutest little mallard I have ever seen."

My grin consumes my face. "You too, Mr. Youngblood. You are the only person I know who can make feathers sexy." I flap my wings in a nonsexy way, making a child clutch his mother's leg as the family passes by. "Quack quack."

I love how Deacon chuckles as he shakes his head like he doesn't know what to make of me.

"Are you ready to kick some duck booty?" He picks me up, making me squeal, then gives me a toe-curling kiss.

And just like that, I am close to forgetting all about the cruise. I could just eat crow and let Dad pay for a trip. That would make him happy, but then I would be indebted to him emotionally, so I will have to tamp down my hormones for a little while longer.

Deacon plants my feet back on the floor, and with a sexy wink, he motions with his head. "Come on, let's show them how it's done."

Hand in hand, we scurry down the concourse, bumping into drunk patrons along the way.

"Sorry," Deacon says as we belt out a laugh. No matter what happens tonight, I've got the best prize in the world staring down at me in a costume covered in feathers. But a cruise would make everything so much better.

Chapter Two

Chrissy

If I don't break my tail on the ice, it will be a miracle. Thank goodness, Deacon catches me each time I get off balance. His strong arms hold me tightly while he graces me with those adorable smiley eyes.

As we and the two other duck-suited couples stand at the center of the ice, I lock eyes with one of the dudes. He points his hand toward his eyes then toward me, indicating he's got his eye on me. Like a mature human being, I stick my tongue out at him. His partner, who isn't as big as a minute, snarls at me. She juts her chin high as she scans the crowd in the arena while the workers drag out three huge plastic bathtubs onto the ice, as well as orange cones.

The announcer takes a microphone and says, "Ladies and gentlemen, it's time."

The crowd screams so loud that I slip on the ice again. All the people in the arena twirl blue Crooner rally towels as the ice girls skate around, working the crowd into a frenzy.

"We have three finalists in the Cruisin' for a Cruise contest. First is Sarah and Duke Jenson from Goodlettsville."

Duke. Of course the dude would have a name like Duke. Sarah and Duke wave to the people in the stands, then Duke snarls at me.

"Next, we have Jessica Sanchez and Bobby Whitmore from Franklin."

They flap their wings as they slip on the ice.

"And lastly, we have Chrissy Parks and Deacon Youngblood from right here in Nashville."

Deacon swivels to me, and we let our beaks touch, pretending we're kissing. I get my bearings and find my father's suite. Even though he probably can't see me, I wave to him anyway.

"If we could get our ice girls to push the tubs to the starting mark, we'll get this contest started."

While the arena erupts in cheers, three girls dressed in shorts so tiny that they really should be at the beach instead of an ice arena slide three big claw-foot bathtubs to the center of the rink. The legs of the tubs have been fitted with ice skate blades.

"Ladies, please climb inside your tubs."

With assistance from the ice girls, we plop down into our tubs. Three other ice girls push out bins, each filled with balloons of one color: red, blue, or green.

"Fill the tubs up with balloons. Remember your color of balloons, because you must not lose any of them. Guys, get behind your tub. You'll push your lady in the tub with the balloons all the way around the rink, staying outside the orange cones. When you make it back to the starting point, you will switch places."

The crowd lets out an infectious cheer.

"Don't forget—you must keep all your balloons. Red tub must have all red balloons. Blue tub with blue balloons, and green tub must have all the green balloons. If any fall out, you must turn your tub around and pick them up."

The crowd groans, and so do I. This is going to be harder than I thought. The first round of this contest a month ago was just how many goals each team could make within a minute. The semifinal round was a fun game of musical chairs on ice. But this round will take some coordination and muscle, two things I lack.

"Are you ready?" the announcer yells into his mic.

The crowd chants, "Go, go, go!" as I sink deep into my tub.

The ice girl dumps the blue balloons all around me, all the time smiling at Deacon. She even bends over to pick up a balloon she dropped on purpose. When our eyes meet, I give her the death stare.

Eyes off my man.

"Guys, push your tubs to the starting mark."

Deacon and the other two dudes slip and slide, doing their best to get traction. Deacon grunts but finally gets our tub to move to the starting point. He leans over to whisper, "Don't move, or else the balloons will fly out."

I nod. "Don't go too fast either."

"Good point."

The announcer yells, "On your mark, get set, go!"

A boom goes off, and the crowd goes wild. Upbeat country music blares through the arena as all three tubs slide on the ice. Duke, my newest nemesis, gains the lead, which ticks me off. But at the first turn, he can't slow the tub down, so they slam into the wall, sending balloons flying everywhere. The other couple takes the lead at the second corner.

I yell as loud as I can to Deacon, "You're going too slow! Hurry!"

Through grunts and groans, he shouts back, "Not as easy as it seems!"

As we make the second turn, the couple in the lead is already at the third turn. Duke slides up beside us.

"Hurry!"

"Don't you move a muscle!" Deacon screams, his face right at my ear. His panting and groaning are loud as he pushes me around in the bathtub.

The first couple makes it to the changing line, but they slide past it, causing them to have to back up, losing a few balloons in the process. Duke and his wife make it to the changing line next, but in her haste, his wife jumps out of the tub, sending balloons all over the rink. Laughter rings throughout the arena.

Deacon slows our tub down and makes a perfectly executed halt at the line. As practiced, I hold my hands up, and Deacon grabs them. He yanks me out of the tub, and the crowd cheers. One foot at a time, he slips into the tub. With all my might, I push against the tub, but my feet slip and slide on the ice.

"Go!" Deacon screams.

"I'm trying."

The first couple gets their tub started as the announcer yells, "Round two. And away we go!"

Duke's wife gets their tub moving, and my hope begins to fade as our tub is the only one left behind. In a calm voice, Deacon says, "You can do this."

Finally, I get some traction, and our tub begins its second trip around the rink. Duke's wife crashes their tub into the wall again, and red balloons fly everywhere. The first couple skates past them. I dig deep into the ice, and with all the energy I can find, I keep a steady, slow pace going.

"Almost there. Stay still, Deacon."

Our tub catches up to the first tub at the third turn.

The guy in the tub sings, "Ice, ice, baby."

I yell, "Kiss my ice!" as they move ahead of us.

"A little faster, sweetie," Deacon says as he sits as low as he can in the bathtub.

The crowd chants, "Go, go, go!"

The dude in the lead tub raises his hands right before they reach the finish line, sending balloons flying all over the rink. Grunting with every push, I do my best not to fall on my duck-suited butt in the process. I give our tub one more push, and we slide across the finish line in first place.

The horn blows, and the crowd goes wild. Cheers are as loud for us as they are when the Crooners score a goal.

Deacon pumps his fist in the air then glances up at me with his sparkly eyes, and with a lopsided grin, he asks, "Can I get out now?"

I giggle. "Yes!"

He jumps out and waddles toward me. I bounce up and down as I slide to meet him.

He wraps his duck arms around me. "We did it."

The announcer pats Deacon on the back, making him slip on the ice. "Deacon and Chrissy, you are the winners of the five-day, four-night, all-expense-paid trip to Bermuda, paid for by our sponsors, Fizzy Girl soda, Great Escape Music, and Step It Up Fitness."

An ice girl skates up to us, holding a big sign that says Cruisin' for a Cruise Winners. So many cameras flash around me that I may see spots in front of my eyes forever.

Into the microphone, the announcer says, "You'll enjoy several days at sea, along with two full days docked at the Royal Navy Dockyard, where you will have plenty of time to explore St. George, snorkel, or swim with the dolphins. Plus, enjoy the fabulous cuisine only Bermuda can offer. You may never want to return."

Deacon slides closer to me and nuzzles my beak with his, making the crowd go "Awww." He is the best boyfriend ever. I never thought I would get him on the ice to begin with, but it was the only way to get him to go on a cruise. He's a landlocked kind of guy. But he loves a good competition.

The announcer holds his hands up to calm the chatter. "I'm not done. It's not just any cruise. It's a theme cruise, and you two have a choice of themes, within reason, of course. Anything from a disco cruise to fitness, to even something more specific. And you'll get five hundred dollars to spend however you want."

My adorable partner's legs buckle, and that ice girl reaches out to grab him, but I swat her hand away. "I got this."

We stand there on the ice and have our picture taken a thousand times, holding a big fake check and a sealed envelope. I wave again in the direction of my father in his company's luxury suite, not knowing if he's even paying attention. But really, I can't wait to get this stupid costume off so that Deacon and I can celebrate in private.

Deacon helps me off the ice, and we are escorted to a locker room to remove our silly costumes. The couples who didn't win follow behind. One guy has sweat trickling down his face while his wife fusses at him the entire way down the concourse. I'm sure all of us can't wait to get out of these horrid, sweaty costumes.

We strip out of the duck suits and toss them into a heap. Deacon slides on a T-shirt over his muscular chest while I hold out the document describing the cruise tickets.

He lets out a chuckle and says, "Ice, ice baby," while he shakes the sweat from his hair.

"I can't believe we did this. I've never won anything in my life. We had better odds at winning the lottery than getting picked to compete, let alone win."

He slides down onto the bench beside me. "Aren't you glad I dragged you to all those games with me instead of sitting up in the snob box? It was our seat number that they picked, remember?"

With my shoulder, I nudge his. "You're going to rub that in for a few years, aren't you?"

He leans down to tie his shoes. "As long as I can get away with it."

"You do know the average weight gain on a cruise is eight pounds."

Deacon shrugs as though it's no big deal. With his metabolism, he could work off any extra weight within a week. "It will be worth every ounce. Just count it as the pounds typically gained during the holidays. What theme do you want to do? Walking Dead or the Knitting Club?"

I belt out a laugh because I didn't even know such bizarre cruises were available. "I have no idea." My brow scrunches as I open the envelope given to me. "Hmm. It looks like we have plenty of time to figure that out. Our cruise date is in May."

"So?"

"That's four months from now."

He wraps an arm around me and pulls me close. Snuggling his nose in my ear, he says, "Sounds like a perfect time for a cruise."

"I just hope we don't hate each other in four months."

Deacon places a hand on each side of my face and lowers his lips to mine in a slow, gentle, but sweltering kiss. I wish we weren't in a hockey locker room that smells like the inside of my brother's gym bag, because I would love to show Deacon how excited I really am. We don't even need to wait to get back to my apartment.

"There is nothing that's going to make me hate you." He leans farther to deepen the kiss, sending us sliding off the bench and onto the floor with him on top of me. "Oof."

"Mr. Youngblood, I hope you are right."

Deacon gazes down at me, and as he dives in for another kiss, my father waltzes in like he owns the place. Dad's scowl makes it obvious he does not approve of what I'm doing or, probably, who I'm doing it with, because behind him is my ex-husband.

Elliot golf claps as he grins down at me and Deacon still sprawled on the locker room floor. Only I would still be buds with my ex, and if we hadn't been joined at the hip since grade school, it would be weird. We found out early on in our marriage that we are definitely better suited to be friends rather than husband and wife. We have an odd, brotherly-love, post-marriage arrangement, and I think it seems to work.

Elliot offers me a hand to stand, which I take. "You two are so disgustingly gushy all the time. But it's cute."

I give him a playful shoulder shove, and out of the corner of my eye, I notice Deacon's demeanor shifts from sexy and fun to stoic and quiet. He's never said anything, but I think he's always been a bit intimidated by the fact that I have a male friend who also happens to be my ex. There's no need to be jealous. Where Elliot is lean like a swimmer with dark, brooding eyes, Deacon has more boyish features with a slice of hunk. Besides, Deacon doesn't get sloppy drunk. In fact, he doesn't drink at all. He doesn't like to "drink his calories," and that's a welcome change for me.

Elliot holds out a hand to shake Deacon's. "Congrats."

Deacon's jaw muscle twitches as he shakes Elliot's hand. His white-knuckled grasp doesn't match his thin smile. "Thanks. Chrissy did all the work." He removes his hand from Elliot's and snakes an arm around my waist, drawing small circles on my hip. I give him a reassuring kiss on the cheek.

My father rolls his eyes. "Priscilla Christine, next time, let me buy you the cruise instead of going through all this nonsense."

My shoulders slump as he sucks all the excitement out of the room. Winning is great, and I'm glad we won, but the point was to do something completely outrageous, something totally out of the box my father likes to put me in. Deacon sees that. Dad never will.

"I think it's fun," Deacon and Elliot reply at the same time.

Take that, Dad.

I slink an arm around Deacon's waist to give him a squeeze, hoping he knows that, of all the testosterone in the room, his is my favorite and I appreciate the way he doesn't care about the money or the status surrounding my family. It's been pure heaven with this man. He loves me as I am with all my flaws, along with my dysfunctional family. Ty plays the part of the perfect son, and Mom is too busy with her clubs and pickleball to even remember she has a family. I can't remember having a decent conversation with my mother in the last year that didn't revolve around how embarrassed of me she still is for divorcing a Whitaker. The nerve!

Deacon makes all the Parks drama fade away. He's perfect for me, and today has been superb. I can't imagine anything changing in the next four months that would put a damper on our trip.

Chapter Three

Deacon - Three Months Later

My one-of-a-kind girlfriend hasn't noticed how nervous I am. If sitting through a green light while staring off into space isn't a sign, the way I keep patting my pocket should be. She is adorable in a strappy sundress, with her soft blond hair snaking down her back in a braid. Those crystal-blue eyes peering through long dark lashes melt me every time, but tonight, something is off.

Chrissy slides her phone back into her pocket faster than she hides her smile. She's been doing that a lot lately, and my Spidey senses go off, trying to figure out what she's up to. I know she's nothing like my ex-girlfriend Angela, because Angela has more secrets than Mookie Betts has major league hits. Something is up, and not knowing is driving me crazy.

"Must be something really interesting," I say as I force my eyes to stay trained on the oncoming traffic. I pat my jacket pocket for the tenth time to make sure I haven't lost the ring box.

"Huh?"

I cut my eyes toward her for an instant before refocusing on the road in front of me. "Your phone. You have smiley eyes."

"I do not."

My hands grip the steering wheel hard enough to break it. If there's anything I hate worse than secrets, it's the lies to cover up the secrets. "That's the fifth text you've received in five minutes. Before dinner is over, you'll have enough to make the beginnings of that romance novel you've wanted to write."

"Pfft. You have an active imagination." She stares out the passenger window, and as we pull into Demo's parking lot, her phone chirps again, causing her to grab it like her life depended on it.

"Can you at least put that on silent mode while we eat?" It's going to be a total buzzkill if her phone ruins what I have planned.

"You're right." She tosses her phone into her purse and opens the car door before I can run around and open it for her. "I'm sorry. I was distracted, and it was rude."

With a kiss to the top of her head, I guide her into the restaurant. The waiter shows us to our table, and behind the menu, I study her face. Her sparkling blue eyes mesmerize me, and her lashes are so long that she doesn't even need mascara. What first caught my attention when we met was her toothpaste-commercial-perfect smile, which complements her constant perky attitude. She can find the good in any situation, and I love everything about her, even when she spouts the most obscure statistics in an otherwise normal conversation.

Sweat trickles down my back as my hand roams into my pocket again.

Her eyes flick up to catch me staring. "What?"

"Just watching you. I like the way you twitch your nose when you're trying to decide on something."

She immediately rubs her nose. "I didn't know I did that."

"It's cute. Don't stop."

Chrissy cocks her head to the side. "Your menu is upside down."

My eyes scan the menu, and she's right. I quickly turn it as a flush creeps up my neck. I am so consumed with what I'm about to do that I'm not even reading the menu.

After I clear my throat, I say, "So, the cruise. Let's talk about it."

She sits up straight in the chair. "Yes, we need to decide on a theme. According to the website, we have five different cruises to choose from that are departing on the day reserved. The deadline to commit is soon."

I sip on my water as I make my final decision on the meal. "Is there anything hideous that we can immediately rule out? I really don't want a bunch of grannies having shuffleboard contests or three-year-olds chasing around a mouse in pants."

Chrissy giggles, which is music to my ears. "Surprisingly, those are not any of the choices." She pulls out a printout and slides it over to me. From her open purse, her cell phone lights up with another incoming message. She peeks into her purse then looks back at the paper. "The five are: fitness and holistic, psychic medium, disco, clothing optional..." Her eyebrows waggle.

My water slides down the wrong pipe, causing me to sputter out a cough. "Are you serious?"

She snickers. "Can you believe that? I don't think I could handle a bunch of floppy boobs roaming around the ship." She does a full-body shiver, and I have to agree with her on this one.

"Or saggy balls." The thought gives me the creeps. "But there could be some really great sagless..."

"Balls?"

"No! Boobs."

She swishes a finger under my nose. "Mister, we are not going on that cruise for you to ogle every pretty bimbo that walks by."

I let out a boisterous laugh, making other customers stare. "I'm kidding. And I certainly don't want other men to gawk at you. You are off limits."

"Trust me, you don't have to worry about me. But I will have to fight the girls... and some guys off of you." Her eyes roam my chest. "You are very easy on the eyes."

I wink as I take her hand in mine to kiss it. "Only for you, sweetie."

"Awww," the server says as she places a basket of bread on our table.

"No thanks. Deacon doesn't eat carbs, right?"

"You know me too well, but I might ease up on my restrictions." I typically steer clear of processed foods and wasted calories as much as possible because I like how healthy eating makes me feel. Plus, I need to be a good role model for my physical therapy clients. "I may allow myself to splurge while on the cruise."

She clasps her hands to her chest. "No way. Mister Iron Man is going to eat... a piece of bread?"

Right before she takes a bite of the roll, I snatch it out of her hand and chomp on it. "I guess I should get my stomach used to the evil ingredients now."

The server stares at us as though trying to decide whether she should leave the basket or take it away. "Uh... your food will be out shortly."

"And don't bother with the dessert menu. The confections industry encourages us to be addicted to their products."

The server glances from me to Chrissy, not knowing what to say. Sometimes, I do get a little preachy with my holistic ideas.

"Don't listen to him." Chrissy addresses our server but rolls her eyes at me. "He's a buzzkill."

"And—"

She holds up a finger to stop my comment. "Do not start about the cycle of obesity."

Our server backs away from our table. "I'm leaving now."

Chrissy leans over the table and stage whispers, "You have got to stop doing that." But the glint of humor in her eyes tells me she's only mildly annoyed at my philosophy.

"Fine. Have it your way." I wink to make sure she knows I'm not mad. Nothing is going to dampen my mood with what I have planned. To change the subject, I say, "You said there are five cruises to choose from, but I got distracted by the last one you mentioned."

"Oh yeah." She picks up the paper again and quirks an eyebrow. "Role Playing."

"Done. That's the one." My eyes dance as I picture her dressed as a sexy nurse or a not-so-innocent prep schoolgirl. The options are endless.

She wiggles in her seat as she pulls out her phone. Maybe she's imagining me dressed as Thor or a police officer with a uniform that will snap off with the slightest flex of my muscles.

With a confident nod, she says, "I have just submitted our choice."

Right as she tosses it back into her purse, her phone buzzes again.

"Go ahead. I know you want to check."

"It's probably work." She rifles through her purse to retrieve her phone.

"Those fortune cookies don't write themselves."

With a smirk, she says, "I'll have you know it's tough coming up with new and catchy fortunes. My boss just increased my quota."

I throw my hands up in defense. "Hey, I think it's a cool career. And you're the perfect person for it."

Her mouth turns down, the face she makes every time her parents cross her mind.

"Too bad my father doesn't have the same enthusiasm for it." She perks up and adds, "Besides, it's a stepping stone. I'm not even thirty yet. I have plenty of time to sort things out."

"That's the spirit. Sometimes, I'd like a creative career instead of rehabbing people's injured knees and ankles."

I do my best to swing the pendulum back toward normal life since she's lived in the world of always doing exactly what the patriarch of the family wants. My family is such a stark contrast to her upbringing that I can only imagine the pressure she's been under to be everything they expect yet always failing.

"Then you wouldn't have met me." The lilt in her words is her doing her best to keep the conversation light.

"That's true."

I think back to when I was assigned this sweet, beautiful woman with a torn anterior talofibular ligament. She worked through her pain by chatting up a storm. Before a month of rehab sessions were done, I knew all about her overbearing, rich father and her nonexistent mother and that she'd recently had the courage to divorce a husband that sounded more like an arranged marriage than anything involving romance. And all of this made me fall in love with her.

"I think your ankle injury wasn't quite as bad as you made out. I'm a professional, remember? I know things."

Her cheeks turn the cutest shade of pink. "Guilty. I figured you would eventually ask me out, but you never did. I did enjoy our time together even when you were making me do painful exercises."

"You didn't want to hobble around the rest of your life, did you?"

With a heavy sigh as she snatches another roll out of the basket, she replies, "You're the best at your job, but you also are the worst at knowing when someone is flirting with you."

"Oh, I knew. I just don't date clients. But I don't have any problem with dating a former one, if she's you."

With a glass held out in a toast, she says, "To role-playing."

I clink her glass with mine, almost spilling my water all over her.

She touches my face. "Are you sweating?"

Yes, but I'm not going to tell her that. I stuff my mouth with a forkful of salad. "Of course not."

"You're warm. Are you feeling alright?" Chrissy places the back of her hand to my cheek.

After I count to three, I clear my throat. *It's now or never.*

"I've been trying to find the right words to tell you this."

Her face blanches as her chest rises and falls. "You're breaking up with me?"

"No!" My volume has three other couples staring at us.

I retrieve the black velvet box out of my pocket and get down on one knee. She drops her fork.

"I love you so much, and I want to spend the rest of my life with you. Will you marry me?" I open the box to reveal the custom-made engagement ring I've been hiding in my drawer for a month.

Her mouth gapes open, but no words come out—no "OMG, yes" or even "of course I will" or a squeal of excitement. At this point, I'll take a simple yes, but she isn't giving me any answer. I feel all eyes on me as my knee bores into the carpet, and the only sound I hear is my heart beating so hard that I feel it's going to explode.

"Uh... Chrissy?"

Her face pales as she swallows hard. Her breaths come out in rapid pants. "I... I... uh, I..." Her chair falls backward as she runs toward the bathroom.

I glance around, and everyone quickly buries their heads in their plates. The restaurant is deathly quiet, and I wish the floor would open up to swallow me whole. I rise slowly and return to my seat as I stuff the ring box back in my pocket. "Just a minor setback," I mumble to anyone paying attention.

Thank goodness the other customers start chatting again, while I try to figure out a way to finish this evening without being completely humiliated.

My phone chimes, and when I pull it out of my pocket, I immediately regret it. Angela hasn't messaged me since she left for rehab a month ago. While I hope she's sober now, I really don't want to have any contact with her.

Knowing I shouldn't answer, I do anyway. I'll do anything right now to keep from overthinking what just happened. "Hey."

"Hey, bud." Angela's voice is steady and sounds completely sober, thank goodness.

"What's up?" I hope this conversation wraps up soon, especially before Chrissy comes back because she is super insecure about my past relationship. I understand. I could say the same thing about me when it comes to Elliot. He's around way too much for me to not have a nagging feeling about him.

"I wanted you to be the first to know I'm out of rehab and feeling a thousand times better, thanks to you."

"I'm glad... for you."

"I wanted to make sure you got the money. While I was away, the early withdrawal from my 401k hit my account. So, thanks for the loan in the meantime. I really didn't trust myself to wait any longer to start the program. You know how it is."

The five thousand dollars I'd loaned her showed up in my account yesterday, and I was floored she actually paid me back. I'd figured I would never see that money again, but it was perfect timing because I needed it for the massive engagement ring, which it seems like I bought for nothing.

"I got it, and thanks for repaying me. It will come in handy."

"Now that I'm out of rehab, I wanted to remind you about being my sponsor."

This is part of my past I have not told Chrissy about, mainly because I never plan to be that person ever again. She's told me many times about how Elliot's personality would change when he drank heavily, and I don't ever want her to think I'm that way too. I was, but not anymore.

When Angela and I were dating several years ago, we were seriously into the party scene: drinking until four o'clock, consuming alcohol first thing in the morning to get the day started, and even blacking out one time. It got out of control, and I almost lost my physical therapy license, so I decided to enter rehab. Part of my lease on a new life meant I needed to stop seeing Angela. She wasn't ready to change then. But when she contacted me, saying she was ready to turn over a new leaf, I felt an obligation to help her even though we weren't together anymore and we wouldn't ever be again.

"Of course. I think this is the start of something good. I'm proud of you."

"Me too. I feel great. But..."

"Go on."

"Are you going to propose to Chrissy?"

The timing of this conversation is not lost on me. I certainly don't want to admit to Angela that I did indeed propose to Chrissy and she fled like a frightened deer. "Maybe soon."

"I hope so, Deacon. I think you two are good together. I mean it."

"Thanks. I gotta go."

After I end the call and take a deep breath, I stand to search for Chrissy. I need to find out why she bailed on me and whether I'm to assume that means she doesn't want to marry me. I peek down the hall-way toward the bathroom, but no one is around, so I scan the kitchen but don't see her there either. My last resort is to walk out to the parking lot. As soon as I exit the restaurant, I spot her standing next to an all-too-familiar black Porche with her hands around the waist of a dude—not just any dude, but Elliot.

My molars grind together as my pulse thumps in my temples.

"You are the best," she says with her back to me.

Elliot looks up, and when he catches my eye, his mouth drops. He stuffs his hands into his pockets and looks from me to Chrissy, who still clings to him like he's her lifeline.

I stand still as if my feet are encased in concrete then clear my throat in an exaggerated way, making Chrissy whip around, her face white as a ghost.

"Deacon."

This cannot be happening. I backpedal into the restaurant, toward our table. If I ate one bite, I would throw it up. The *clickity-click* of Chrissy's shoes is my warning that she's following me.

"Deacon, wait."

I throw a hand up to stop her from saying anything else. "Let me guess. All the texts were from him."

"Yes, but—"

My heart drops in my stomach, and I think I'm going to be sick. Maybe our relationship was one-sided, and she didn't feel the same for me as I thought she did. Sometimes, the green monster crept into our conversations, but she would always quell my insecurities. But now, my suspicions were spot on. "I need to get out of here."

With one swift move, I toss some money on the table and proceed out of the restaurant, head hanging low, doing my best not to overreact.

Chrissy does her best to keep up with me. "Wait. Let's talk."

"Actions speak louder than words, Chris."

I click my key fob to unlock my car and hold the passenger door open for Chrissy to climb in.

"Please, let me explain."

After three attempts, I finally get my seatbelt fastened. I crank my beat-up Chevy Impala and grind it into reverse. "I don't want to talk right now. I might say something—"

"I'm not cheating."

"Interesting that your mind went there immediately." I blow out a breath and wait in silence to see if Chrissy says anything. When she doesn't, I ask, "Is he why you ran away from me when I proposed?"

"What? No. Not at all. Well, sort of." She slumps back in the seat and groans while running her hands over her face.

My heart hurts, and I'm two seconds away from breaking down in front of her. "I can't believe this is happening." I mumble my words because I'm mainly thinking out loud.

She touches my arm, making my forearm muscles flex. "You know my marriage crashed and burned before I made it to my paper anniversary. I don't want to do that again unless I am one hundred percent certain this time."

"And you aren't certain. Is that what you're saying?"

She swallows as she removes her hand from my arm. I already miss the contact. "I... I can't explain."

"Are you afraid I won't be accepted into the Parks family? Do I not make enough money? What is it, Chris? Are you not over *him*?" These words are definitely meant for her ears, and she knows exactly who I am referring to. Him: the third wheel in this relationship.

I hate that she takes forever to answer. The truth feels like it slips through the silence. After a few deep sighs, she finally says, "You have to know I am completely over Elliot and he has nothing to do with what is going on. Besides, he's just a friend. Nothing more."

White-knuckled, I zoom toward our apartment, the blood rushing so quickly in my head that I can't hear anything. I know she's rambling on about something, but it's all incoherent babble to me. When I reach our apartment, I open my car door even before the engine stops sputtering, winding down. Chrissy follows me inside and collapses onto the couch. I find my gym bag and toss clothes into it.

She jumps up and stands in front of me. "What are you doing?"

"I should leave."

"No. Let's talk."

Clenching my jaw, I fight the urge to sit down and yell, afraid I will say hurtful things, words I won't be able to take back. Nonverbally, I chant the mantra that helped me at the beginning of my sober life: "Breathe, Deacon. Just breathe." Once I've gone over a thousand options, I reply, "Maybe later."

Hurt flashes across her eyes. "Maybe? Like *maybe* we can talk later, or *maybe* we won't?" Her pain switches to anger in a flash. "I choose the latter."

We stand there, our eyes glued to one another. I'd only wanted a night to stay at my brother's house to calm down, but now, this feels like it's the end for us. "Well, it looks like you get your wish."

"If you had trusted me—"

I cut off her words with an evil chuckle while I rake a hand through my hair. "You were wrapped around your ex-husband. You were texting him, right? For all I know, you were sexting him. You betrayed *my* trust too many times. In the back of my head, I knew it was more than friends." I hate using air quotes.

"You want to talk about trust? Are you going to tell me you haven't spoken to Angela?" She crosses her arms and taps her toe, waiting for me to answer.

"Don't start with her. I'm not the one who did anything wrong here."

While she plunks down on the couch, I pat my pocket to make sure I still have the ring. I retrieve it and open the box to inspect the one-of-a-kind, pear-shaped engagement ring. The lavender sapphire center stone—her favorite—surrounded by diamonds took a lot of planning, but I thought she was worth it. When the clerk asked if I wanted to purchase a refund policy, I laughed at how ridiculous the idea of ever needing to return it sounded. *Who's laughing now?*

After another moment, I snap the box closed then stuff it back in my pocket. Entering the bedroom, I snatch my memory foam pillow off the bed and notice the cruise information perched on her nightstand.

From the other room, she says, "Are you going to tell me you haven't been talking to Angela behind my back?"

I let out a deep sigh. I have, but it's not like she thinks. Besides, that doesn't even matter anymore. "She owed me money." I should tell her why, but then I would have to confess about being a recovering alcoholic, and right now, that would only make things worse, so I don't give her any more details—not my finest moment, but I'm too hurt to have this argument projected back on me.

I snatch the cruise information and shove it into my pocket as I walk back into the living room.

"She owed you money. For what? Services rendered?"

"Cute." She doesn't deserve any additional reply.

She juts her chin in the air, and at this moment, she resembles the way her father always looked at me: smug, entitled, upper-crust. "Never mind. I don't want to know."

"I'll get the rest of my stuff when you're at work tomorrow, coming up with the latest quirky fortune."

Chrissy pins me in place with her sneer. Never have I ever made fun of her career until now. I know she's considered a laughingstock among her father's social circles, and for me to add that insult is too low. I turn in circles, taking in the apartment we've shared over the last four months. A part of me wants to drop my bag and reset this entire night, but I think it's gone too far now to turn back.

"Goodbye." I close the door but force myself not to slam it. Anger management is one of the many things I had to work through during rehab, and I'm being tested right now.

As I wait impatiently for my cranky car engine to turn over, Chrissy crashes out the front door.

"Did you take the printout about the cruise?"

I smile as my car sputters to life, then I roll down the window—yes, my car is *that* old—and put my hand to my ear like I didn't hear her. Just to get her goat, I bat my eyes. "I don't have a clue what you're talking about."

She reaches into my car, and I playfully smack her hand before she grabs the paperwork out of my front pocket.

"Deacon, you better not even think about going on that cruise with me."

"I recall being part of the winning team. See you on deck."

She backs up and plants her hands on her hips with a huff. As I drive away, I recall how quickly this night went from cozy to chaotic. I should have let her have the cruise tickets. If not for her, I would never have gotten on the ice to begin with. Even if my seat did get selected, I would've let someone else take my place. Relinquishing my ticket to her would be the right thing to do, but there is no way on Earth I'm going to let her share my stateroom with her ex-husband. I'd rather be stuck on the *Titanic* with her than let her have any sexy times with that twenty-first-century Eddie Haskell.

Chapter Four

Chrissy

His taillights grow dim, leaving me in the parking lot alone with my thoughts. I can't believe two hours ago, everything was fine. It was more than fine. It was as great as it always has been until I freaked out about his proposal. I have no idea why I did so, except maybe I'm gun shy. I've walked down the aisle once in haste, and I don't want to make another mistake.

Then Elliot showed up. He has the worst timing ever. If I had been in Deacon's shoes, I might've connected those dots also. I only wish he'd listened to me before my big mouth got going faster than my brain.

Like a zombie, I stumble back inside to glance around at our apartment. It already feels lonely and quiet with Deacon gone. Most of his things are still here, but he isn't, and I miss him already. It's too quiet. All of this could have been avoided if I had just said yes. That shouldn't have been so hard to say.

Apparently, it was. When Elliot proposed, he did it in front of five hundred people at the Swan Ball. With both my parents beaming like proud peacocks, I couldn't refuse. And when Deacon popped the question, I froze. I love him. There's no doubt about my feelings, but I don't know if I'll ever be ready to make that kind of commitment again.

I flop down on the couch and let out a deep sigh as I try to figure out what just happened. Before I can curl up into a ball, tears flow down my cheeks, and my breath hitches. The accusations he threw my way and the things I said to him can't be unsaid. I sniffle and wipe the tears off my face as I squint to focus on my cell phone. Tears make my display such a blur. I should remove my contacts because they're going to float out of my eyes before long.

Scrolling through the pictures on my phone, I get to the ones from the contest. He was adorable, even in a fluffy yellow suit. If I didn't know it before, I knew it that day: I was totally in love with him. Then, today happened, and I ruined everything.

The only person who can help me is my best friend, so I call April. We've been friends since kindergarten and have endured debutante balls, numerous boyfriends, and college, and she was even my maid of honor. If I'd listened to April in the first place, I wouldn't have been divorced by the age of twenty-five. The first moment she met Deacon, she put her seal of approval on him, so she's the only one that can help me figure out what to do next. Hopefully, she won't get her husband, my brother, involved. If Ty knows, Dad will know, and I'll get the "told you so" lecture of a lifetime.

When she sees my face on the phone screen, her brow scrunches. "Whoa. What's going on?"

Trying to catch my breath and talk at the same time is not easy. "He... left... me."

"What are you saying?" she screeches through the phone.

"He's gone." The words don't even sound like they came from my throat. I never in a million years thought Deacon would leave me.

"I'll be right over."

"April—"

But before I can protest, she disconnects the phone, and I'm staring at the wall. I get up to wander into the bedroom and slink down onto Deacon's side of the bed. An indentation where he slept the night before is still there. His pillow is gone, but the sheets still smell like him. His musky scent wafts over my tear-drenched face. If I hadn't been such a jerk to him, maybe we could've talked this out. Going over the shoulda-coulda-wouldas puts me in a daze that only the banging on my front door is able to jerk me out of.

God, I hope that's Deacon. Maybe he's regretting everything too. Right now, I want nothing more than to have a reset and start this night over.

I rush to the door and fling it open, but it's not him. April and my brother, Ty, stand in front of me, and my shoulders sag as my last hope deflates. They rush into the apartment without even a second thought.

Where I favor my mother, with blond hair and a free spirit, Ty is all Dad, complete with his broad shoulders and business mind. My only complaint with him is that I have to share my best friend with him. April is pretty awesome and already knew the ridiculous family she was getting involved with when they got together, so I'm okay with sharing.

Ty's nostrils flare as he paces my living room. "What's going on, PC? Do you want me to beat him up? If he cheated on you—"

April holds out a hand to stop him. "He's not a cheater, so just catch your breath and let Chrissy fill us in." She looks at me. "He didn't cheat on you, did he?"

I slide down onto the couch, and they flank me, so we are all shoulder to shoulder. "No... but... he thinks I did. And... he proposed, and I flaked and..." I bury my head in my hands. "Oh, the things we said to each other. It was awful."

Ty wraps his arms around me and holds me to his chest. "Back up. I just saw you two a few days ago, and he couldn't keep his hands off you, and you certainly weren't putting up a fight."

April leans her head on my shoulder and pats my leg. "You two are nauseatingly affectionate."

Ty laughs, making my head bob up and down on his chest. "It's disgusting. No two people should be into each other that much."

"Hey, now. Your wife is right here." April points at herself then looks over at me. "If he would work less, he might see he's got a hot babe at home, ready and willing to do all kinds of fun things."

Ew. Thinking of my brother doing stuff with my bestie is not what I want to have running through my mind right now. "Guys, you can do that at home."

April nods. "You're correct. Back to you and Deacon. Did you say he proposed? That's fantastic."

I show her my left hand, which is devoid of an engagement ring. "No, it isn't fantastic. When he whipped out the ring in the restaurant, I froze. All I could think about was that I was going to make a mistake again."

Ty shakes his head as he tsks me. "Way to rush to condemn the marriage before the ink is dry on the license."

He's right, but that's not the point. "You know most marriages end in divorce. Throw a second one on top, and it's destined to fail."

April hugs me, making me feel a tiny bit better, but not really. "You don't know that. Your marriage to Elliot was built on like, not love. Both of you tried to put on a happy face, but it was destined to fail. Just know that Deacon is not Elliot."

Ty crosses one ankle over the other as he rests his feet on my coffee table. "Why does he think you cheated on him?"

My nerves are getting the best of me. I nibble on a fingernail because what I'm about to say sounds worse than it really is. "Because I was secretly meeting with Elliot."

"What?" The screeches from both of them are deafening. They sit up, almost bumping heads as they stare at me.

"Sis, why on earth would you do that?"

"I'm not cheating with Elliot or anyone else. I was trying to surprise Deacon for his birthday."

April cringes. "With what? A sex tape of you with your ex?"

Ew. "That's disgusting. I heard Dad say Elliot was selling his season tickets to the Crooners, and I wanted to buy them for Deacon."

My brother leans over me to stage-whisper to his wife. "April, if you ever want to noncheat with Elliot to get his tickets, you have my permission."

April gives him the death stare then focuses back on me.

"Tonight, at dinner, he texted me a dozen times that he had another offer for the sale, and I had to lie to Deacon about who it was."

As usual, Ty makes himself at home and wanders into the kitchen to retrieve one of Deacon's Perrier bottles from the refrigerator. "I take it he read the messages?"

"No. Deacon would never do that. We don't sneak around and look at private stuff. I don't read his emails or texts, and he's never seen mine. And there was never anything to hide from him before this. I promise—Elliot and I are just buds."

I tuck a stray strand of hair behind my ear and take a deep breath. "That's not the worst. Elliot showed up at the restaurant. I went into full panic mode. I didn't want Deacon to see him and think more than what it was, so I snuck out to the parking lot to meet Elliot. The next thing I knew, Deacon was standing there. His face was red, and I thought he was going to hyperventilate. He thinks I wigged out on the proposal because I still have feelings for Elliot."

Ty mumbles something under his breath. The only words I can make out are not flattering. This conversation isn't helping me. I fling my hands in the air and stand to pace the room, taking Ty's bottle away from him. I take a huge swig before finishing my story. "It gets worse." I cringe because this is going to sound terrible, and I don't know how they will react. "Deacon caught me hugging Elliot."

Ty stares at his wife. "Uh-oh."

With my hands out in defense, I add, "To be fair, I went in for a side hug, and Elliot took it as an opening to do a full-body embrace. It was awkward at best, and I didn't know what to do."

April rubbed my shoulder. "Didn't you set the record straight?"

I shrugged. "It was a lame attempt, but things got out of hand quickly. He said things. So did I. I even accused him of cheating with his ex-girlfriend, Angela." I point my finger toward Ty. "But come to think of it, he did admit he had been talking to her."

"That's not cheating," April says. Even now, she's team Deacon.

"But he kept it from me."

Ty stares at the ceiling and lets out a huge groan. "Maybe he had a good reason, the same as you."

With one large gulp, I finish off the remainder of the sparkling water then place the bottle on the coffee table, Deacon's table. "It doesn't matter. Now, we have a cruise coming up, and we might push each other off the boat if we have to spend any time on the same ship."

"Why don't you let us take your tickets?" April grins and stares at Ty.

He winks and nods at his wife. "I think that's a fantastic idea."

"Very funny. I won those tickets, so I'm going. Besides, when he stormed out earlier, he took the info, so I know he'll be going just to annoy me. And it's a themed cruise. We chose..." I nibble on a fingernail, wondering if I should continue. "We chose role-playing." I cringe at how creepy that sounds.

"Let him go on that one, and you go on a different one."

I love the way my brother thinks, but that wouldn't work. "It's one stateroom, so it has to be the same cruise."

April takes a deep breath. "Okay, so go. Have the time of your life, but you should pick a different theme, something only you want, not him."

"I locked in our choice, so we're stuck."

April grins. "We should go shopping for a sexy nurse outfit. You know... just in case." She winks, and I fight back a grin. It's the first time I've felt like smiling this evening.

Ty groans as a blush creeps up his neck. "Girls. I think this is a bad idea. You need to call Deacon right now and clear the air. It doesn't matter if you ruined tonight. You need to think of the big picture."

He's right. I need to find where Deacon is staying tonight and make him listen to me. I don't want to have this conversation over the phone. Once we have a chance to calm down and talk it out in person, he'll realize nothing was happening, and we can have the time of our life on the cruise together.

Since I'm thinking more clearly now, the best thing I can do is call Deacon and hope he will be willing to reconcile or at least meet up to chat. I pull my phone out and call Deacon's number, but my hope fades immediately. "Oh no."

April scrunches her brow. "What is it?"

My heart sinks into my stomach. When I can form words again, I say, "It rang one time then went straight to voice mail. You don't think he…"

Ty sucks in a breath through his teeth. "I think so."

Someone knocks on the door. I bolt off the couch. "Maybe that's Deacon." I fling the door open to see Elliot standing there, hands stuffed in his pockets. My shoulders sag when reality hits me. I poke him in the chest. "Worst timing ever, El."

Elliot follows me into my living room, where he nods at Ty. "Chris, I am so sorry. I clearly messed up something important tonight. What happened?"

Ty nudges him into a chair and paces in front of him like he's holding court. "Let me give you the abridged version of this sordid tale. Dea proposed. Chrissy freaked. Then you showed up. Deacon put two and two together to make ten. He thinks you are the reason she didn't say yes."

My ex-husband's jaw drops as he gazes around at us. "That wasn't it at all."

April sneers down at him. She's never liked him much, and this last fiasco solidifies her opinion of him. "And it is kind of your fault."

"Me?" He stares at each of us.

I groan and shake my head. "No. It's all *my* fault, but when you showed up at that exact moment, it did not win me any points, that's for sure."

He throws his hands in the air. "I had to know immediately if you really wanted the tickets. I had three other offers breathing down my neck for them too. If you weren't serious, I needed to pounce on the next in line."

We sit in silence, and I relive the mess I'm in. I believe Elliot, but if he'd just left it with a brotherly side hug, I might've been able to talk to Deacon about my hesitancy.

Ty slides an arm around my shoulder and gives me a slight squeeze. "Now, my sweet sister will be on a cruise with Deacon, and get this: It's a role-playing cruise." He waggles his eyebrows for added emphasis.

Elliot blinks, trying to process Ty's comment. "I'm sorry, what?"

I shrug. "You heard him. We leave next month on the sixth on the *Sovereign of the Sea* for a five-day cruise to Bermuda." I pull up the cruise info on my phone and show it to him. "We depart from Miami."

"Are you still going?"

"Yep."

"Hmm." Elliot stares off. "You're brave. Or stupid. I'm not sure which."

If he weren't speaking the truth, I would be offended, but I don't have a comeback to that. While Elliot and Ty chat about something work related, April helps me pick out some costumes online—bad idea, but I see no reason to start making good decisions this late in the day.

Chapter Five

Deacon

It doesn't take my little brother Drake even two seconds to call in re-inforcements. I should've gone to a hotel to give my brain time to calm down, but instead, I end up at his bachelor pad. He hasn't evolved much since college, and I wonder how much action the couch I'm sitting on has seen. On second thought, maybe I don't want to know.

My sister, Bailey, and brother Aaron and his wife and kids gather around me like it's story time at the old Youngblood home. This is not a tale to be retold at family reunions. I don't even want to tell it once. But if not for my family, I would be nowhere. We support each other through everything. From Aaron and Claire's troubled start to Bailey's miscarriage and my rehab, we never leave each other hanging, so I guess it's my turn for their support.

Drake clangs on his beer bottle with the opener. "The Youngblood meeting has come to order." He points at Aaron's toddlers, Ezra and Farrin, and says, "Hey, kiddos, scoot. Disney channel is on in my bedroom."

That's all it takes since Aaron and Claire give them only thirty minutes of screen time per day at home.

When they're safely out of listening range, Drake waves to me. "Tell them."

Bailey hovers next to me, and her big blue eyes fill with concern. "Tell your big sister everything."

After I spill my guts and fight off some embarrassing tears, I prop my elbows on my knees and bury my head in my hands. "I really thought she would want to marry me."

Aaron lounges in the recliner, staring at the ceiling. He chews on the side of his mouth like he's trying to find the right words. "Don't you think you might have overreacted a bit?"

From one sibling to another then my sister-in-law, I look at my family. Everyone glances away, but Aaron's wife cringes and says, "I normally stay out of Youngblood family stuff, but I'll horn in this time. I think you're right to be upset. You expressed your undying love in a very public way and got shot down, then *he* shows up. I can see where you made the 'leap.'"

I sigh out loud, but she throws out a hand before I can say anything.

"And I would have been furious too, but to pack a bag and leave like that was over the top. Don't you think you went a little bit overboard?"

"Nope. She was cuddling with her ex-husband. What am I supposed to do? If I shrug it off once, it'll happen over and over."

Bailey rolls her eyes. "Chrissy is the real deal. And you're different with her. You love her."

"Not anymore."

With a chuckle under his breath, Aaron shakes his head. "Dude, you were under her spell from the first time you met her. You can't just turn your feelings off with a switch like *I* can."

Bailey nods in agreement with our big brother. "I remember you telling me when you first laid eyes on her. You were tongue-tied. Couldn't put three words together to form a simple sentence."

Heat rushes up my neck. "That is a bit of an exaggeration."

Aaron gives me a knowing look, and arguing is futile. They're right. To use an old phrase, I was smitten.

"Bro, don't be an idiot."

Maybe I am being rash. It could all be a big misunderstanding. I never even considered reading her emails or text messages. It's not my style. And up until tonight, I didn't have a reason to even think she was cheating. But she was in his arms. That's so not cool.

"She didn't try too hard to deny it or to get me to stay so we could talk it out. She just sat there and threw barbs my way."

Drake whistles as he hands me a bottle of Coke, which I gladly take. "What did she say?"

"She wanted to know if I was seeing Angela again."

"But—"

I cut Bailey off because I know what she's going to say. "Yes, I saw Angela, but it was for a very good reason, and I am not cheating. I don't do that."

Drake wiggles his left hand under my nose, and I swat it away. "Are you going to return the rock?"

"I can't. It's custom made, so that's thousands of dollars down the drain. I guess I could sell it on eBay."

Claire jumps up, startling all of us. "Stop." She paces the living room and yanks the Coke bottle out of my hand and takes a swig. "You have been with this wonderful girl for almost a year, and you want to just give up. Do you even hear yourself?"

Tears burn my eyes, so I squeeze them shut, begging them to stay in place. If I cry in front of Drake, I'll never hear the end of it.

"I agree with Claire." Bailey smiles at our sister-in-law. "There has to be a perfectly good reason for all of this, and you owe it to yourself and to her to get to the bottom of it."

Aaron nods. "Hey, don't you two have a cruise coming up?"

I flop back and rest my head against the couch. "Yes, and I took the travel information with me, so no matter what happens, I'm on that ship. With or without her."

Bailey pops me on the shoulder. "That's the spirit. Make her forget this little tussle." She cocks her head to the side. "You know exactly what you need to do."

Drake grins at me like what I should do is give him the ticket. *Not happening.* "What should I do?"

Claire rolls her eyes and looks at Bailey. "Are all the Youngblood boys this dense?"

"Apparently." Bailey turns back to me. "You need to go on that cruise and win her back. She freaked when you proposed, but you overreacted. You both said things you didn't mean. There are clearly some misunderstandings that need to be ironed out. Use the cruise to fix it. You'll be forced to spend time together. And the best part is you can't just jump ship if she makes you angry. You'll have to work it out."

Drake stands and says in an announcer voice, "All in favor, raise your hand."

Four hands rise. After I take in each expression, I let out a defeated sigh.

Aaron says, "Dude, you're not going to win this argument."

My phone chirps, and for a fleeting second, I hope it's Chrissy, but it can't be her because, like a fool, I blocked all contact with her. I take out my phone and groan. "Oh no."

Not wanting to believe this is happening to me, I toss my phone to Bailey. "It's Angela."

Drake chuckles. "Bro, you are toast."

"I promised to be her sponsor, but I assumed she would wing it even though that's not how any of this works."

Bailey snoops and reads my other emails. When she reads one message, her eyes grow wide as she bounces in her seat. She doubles over in a fit of giggles. "Role-playing?" She hides my phone so I can't snag it out of her grip.

Rumbles of laughter make Aaron almost fall out of the recliner. "Are you going to be Bo Bo, the pool boy?"

Snatching my phone back, I find the link to the cruise and go to the Edit link. My heart sinks when I see our cruise of choice has been confirmed. No switcheroos.

"It won't let me change it."

Drake pops me on the back as a rumble of laughter bubbles out of his throat. "Dude, with or without Chrissy, it's role-play. Listen to me carefully. Go and have fun... playing."

I'm in love with a girl who isn't being truthful with me. I have to decide what I really want and how much I'm willing to fight for it or if it's time to cut my losses. Loving a person who doesn't love back at the same level is painful, especially at first, but I need to move forward. I stand and roll my head side to side to loosen my stiff muscles. "Bro, you are completely right. I'm a free man."

Claire puts her hands on her hips and huffs. "Drake, you're the one who's a bad influence on him. We're talking about love, not lust."

He rolls his eyes then turns to me. "Forget Chrissy. If you don't update me every single hour, I'm going to punch your lights out. This is better than winning the lottery."

Aaron shoves Drake out of the way. "While I mostly agree with Drake—"

Claire gasps. "I'm going to remember you said that."

He continues, "You do need to at least try to make it right with Chrissy while you're there. If it doesn't work out, at least you know you tried."

I nod, knowing he's right. It's all fun and games with Drake, but Aaron is more of the romantic. I already miss everything about Chrissy. I miss her smile, her giggle, the soft way she sighs when she snuggles next to me in bed. I have to at least try to reconcile, and the cruise is the perfect setup.

My phone buzzes again with an incoming FaceTime. Angela's number pops up on my screen.

"I should see what she wants."

Claire and Bailey grab for my phone, but I hold it high out of their reach while I walk out the front door to have some quiet while I take the call. Once I'm out of my meddling family's earshot, I answer the call.

"Hey, Angela."

She's usually put together, but today, her hair is brassy, and she doesn't have a stitch of makeup on, clearly a sign that something is off with her. "Oh, thank goodness you picked up. My first day back at work, and they fired me."

"Can they do that? You weren't goofing off this past month. You were getting sober."

"Yeah, they can, especially since I told a very high-profile client to take a hike because they didn't like my design ideas. I couldn't take the edge off with a noontime cocktail, and my anger got the best of me."

I run a hand through my hair. "There's a lot of that going around. Chrissy and I broke up."

"What happened? I talked to you earlier today, and you said you were going to propose."

"I did. Actually, I don't want to talk about it."

In a soft voice, she says, "I'm really sorry. She never liked me, but I thought she was perfect for you. It's something I came to terms with in rehab. Some people are in my life for a reason and only for a season. You weren't long-term for me, but I know that's what she is to you, and I'm okay with that."

I've had enough talk therapy for one day. All I want to do is find a hotel room and crash for a year. "Back to your situation. Did you have anything to drink?"

"Nope, but it was super hard. I'm glad you're my sponsor. I hate to admit it, but I'm going to be calling you constantly for a while."

I remember when I felt like I was bugging my sponsor—seems like just yesterday. Jake was so kind and patient with my every question and worry. I made it through the tough times, and Angela can too. Occasionally, I still feel the need to call Jake, and he always answers. I owe her the same chance at sobriety.

"I'm only a call away. Don't be surprised if you hear a large ship's horn in the background because I'm headed to Bermuda on the fourteenth for five days. The *Sovereign of the Sea*." I roll my eyes at how lame that sounds.

She gasps. "Bermuda? I won't be able to make it that long without some help. I'm already feeling twitchy."

Worst. Timing. Ever.

"We signed the agreement that I could call you at least once a day at least for the next month," she says. "It's obvious you've never been on a cruise. When you're out in the middle of the ocean, your phone doesn't work. You can get a Wi-Fi package, but calling is completely useless. And do you really think Chrissy will think it's totally cool with me being so needy when she doesn't even know about your struggles?"

When Angela sent me the information about being her sponsor, I never considered the fact that I would be gone. I just signed the agreement blindly, thinking that, after the first week, I'd email her every now and then, and that would be it.

Her breath hitches, and I close my eyes, trying to figure out a plan while I'm gone. "Can my brother be a stand-in?"

"You know as well as I do that he'll be a bad influence on me. I've partied hard a few too many times with him in the past. And he hasn't been in the program. It has to be someone who has experienced the challenges."

I knew that, but I was hoping we could skate past that rule for one week. That would get me off the hook but wouldn't be fair to her, and for her sake, I want her to stay sober. She needs this chance.

The way her voice quivers sends a pang of guilt through me.

"You could always be a stowaway," I say.

She gasps, and at first, she sounds disgusted by my not-so-authentic suggestion, but then she says, "That's a great idea."

My head snaps back from the shock of her words. "I was kidding."

"I'm not." After a brief pause, she adds, "Are you leaving from Miami? Role-playing?" Her question is laced with humor.

"How did you know that?"

"Google."

"Well, it was a good idea at the time. And I'm going to try to win Chrissy back, so she doesn't need to get the wrong idea if she runs into you."

"I won't get in the way. I'll stay in my cabin or by the pool." She squeals. "The spa. I need that. Done."

"Wait, you just got fired. How are you going to pay for this?"

"For some strange reason, there are a bunch of staterooms still available, and they seriously slashed the prices. I'll put it on my credit card and worry about it later."

With that, I slump down on Drake's front doorstep and let out a groan. "This is a bad idea."

"It's done. And I will help you win her back."

Even worse idea. "Pfft. I don't know about that."

"I think it's time for us to turn over new leaves. See you on board."

"Wait." My phone goes blank as she cuts off our FaceTime. I slog back into the living room as four sets of beady eyes await me. After I clear my throat, I say, "It looks like this cruise will be a threesome."

Drake drops his beer. Aaron rolls into a fit of giggles, while Claire's and Bailey's mouths fall open.

"Poor choice of words."

Chapter Six

Chrissy
Day One of the Cruise

My research paid off because my flight landed last night and I'm not in panic mode looking for my ship at Port Miami. To call this place huge does not begin to describe it. On one long side, all the cruise ships dock. Their massive structures, one after another, tower so high above me that I am in awe at how they don't topple over, but now is not the time to dive into statistics on sinking ships. Massive cargo ships line the other side as far as the eye can see, with rows of freight waiting to be sent out into the country.

The smell of sea air wafts over me as the seagulls dive for their morning feast. They don't seem fazed by the horns blasting all around. As I wait in line to board the *Sovereign of the Sea*, I triple check that I have my cruise documents and passport easy to retrieve. I don't want to be the passenger who holds up the line by being unprepared.

The wind whips around me, making my blue miniskirt fly up around my waist. April helped me pick this costume out. She said I would make a splash dressed as a sexy sailor, but as much as I like the skirt with the cute blue suspenders, the striped midriff blouse shows off a bit more skin than I'm used to. I force my logical brain to take a hike because I'm on vacation. It's time to have fun, and besides, no one I know will be on board, so I can do whatever I want without any snide comments.

Before I enter the queue to board the massive vessel, I pull out my phone and FaceTime April. When she appears on my screen, I wave.

"I'm here, and I thought I would call one last time before I hit the high seas." I turn in circles to show her my view. "I can't believe I've never been on a cruise before."

"You will have so much fun, and I love your outfit," she says with a saucy wink.

To give her the full view of what I'm wearing, I hold my phone high then squish my lips together in a duck pose. That makes her giggle, and I miss her so much. "I wish you were here. We would have a blast together."

She waves me off. "I'm an old married woman now. My idea of fun is a frozen pizza and a ten o'clock bedtime. I live vicariously through you. Go have fun. Let me know if you meet any interesting people on board."

"You'll be the first I tell anything fun to, but please, keep anything stupid from my brother. Promise?"

April holds up a pinkie as if we were going to perform a childhood promise ritual, and I return the gesture. "See you in a week."

"Don't do anything I wouldn't do. On second thought..." She flashes me a cheesy grin.

A ship's horn blows in the distance, startling me. "I should go. Love ya."

"Love ya more."

The queue to embark is long, but we move at a decent clip, far faster than boarding my flight to Miami. In line in front of me, a guy about my age wears a leather skirt, vest, and belt. He gives me a dirty look as he taps his foam sword against his leg.

A sword? Wait! A Viking helmet too?

Most of the people in line around me seem more like they are on their way to a Ren Faire. All that's missing is a very large turkey leg. I must be in the weirdo line because everyone around me is decked out in period clothing, with even more swords. Lots. None of their costumes scream sexy times, but to each his own.

Surely, they can't bring weapons on board.

Someone bumps me from behind, and when I turn around, I end up with a face full of arrows from a quiver. Thank goodness they're the foam Nerf type. Otherwise, I may have had my first injury of the cruise. I would like to go one day without harming a body part. That's not too much to ask.

Over the intercom, a person bellows, "This is a Parlour Camp."

The guy in front of me slumps his shoulders and lets out a massive groan.

"If you plan to boffer, you must have your weapons approved by going to Gate C."

Almost everyone in the line groans as they schlep down the plank toward a different loading dock. I don't have a clue what "parlour" is, but as long as those boffer thingies are well away from me, I like it. And I'm thrilled that the line is almost nonexistent now.

As I bump up the line of the gangway, flute music trickles down from the deck. From this angle, the ship seems to go for miles toward the sun. Tons of people are already milling around the many decks. Some wave to people at the port, and I wave back, not caring that I don't know anyone. We're all here to have a good time.

A flash of black-and-purple hair catches my attention as a female struts across one of the decks closer to the water's edge. A yoga mat is slung across her shoulder. The last thing I'm going to waste my time onboard doing is exercising.

When I reach the top, I hand my information and passport to the steward. "Welcome to the LARP Boat." He checks my passport against my ticket information and verifies everything matches.

"Excuse me. Did you say Love Boat?"

He shakes his head slowly. "You are in stateroom 6405 in that direction. All alone?"

Yes. No. Maybe. "My... companion will be here soon, I suppose."

He hands my information back, and I snatch it out of his hand and prance toward the bow of the ship. A college-aged guy with a camera around his neck is taking photos of people as they board. He looks like he should be holding a surfboard instead of a camera. "Ma'am, do you want a picture?"

"No, that's okay."

Zack, if his name badge is his real name, smiles. "I get it. Waiting for your partner, right? He must be a PC."

"No, I'm PC, but how did you know my nickname? Only my father calls me PC, so please don't do that."

His eyes rake over me, and I wish I had worn sweatpants and a large T-shirt instead of this barely there getup. "Anyway, it's just me... and Francois, the pool boy." I motion toward my bag with the paperback romance novel peeking out. "But that's our little secret."

"Well, that's rad. Lit costume, by the way." He snaps to attention and salutes me. He snickers then adds, "I hope you and Francois enjoy your cruise. And watch out for the magic dust."

That sounds odd, but I don't care. I've researched everything available on this ship, and if I'm not taking in a live show or shopping, I'll be parked at one of the many pools, soaking up some sun while reading about Francois. Then I have Sanchez, the billionaire, to keep me company if I whip through the pool-boy novel. The ship has tons of things I want to try, and I won't have enough time to do all the shore excursions. Even though I made a list of all the things I want to do, I should take tonight and make a plan.

"I actually am looking forward to all the activities."

Zack belts out a laugh. "You will get your fill of it. That's for sure." He leans in and whispers, "I call this the bizarro cruise, but it pays the bills."

I smirk at him and see another man dressed like he works on the ship, so I stop to ask for help. "Could you help me find my stateroom?"

"Absolutely. That's what I'm here for." He takes a look at my ticket and motions with his head for me to follow him down three levels to level six. "You have an oceanfront view. The stateroom has its own veranda."

He drags my luggage as I follow behind him like a puppy, taking in all the sights and sounds. If I didn't know we were floating, I would swear I was in the most massive mall in the world. The tiled walkway takes us through so many shops that I lose count. Above me is an LED screen showing an enormous shark swimming by. I wonder who thought that was a good idea. The only thing missing is the song from *Jaws* blaring throughout the ship.

I'm so consumed with absorbing everything I see that I have to run to catch back up with the guy who has my luggage. I point at a slide that starts at the top of the ship and winds its way all the way down to the deck we're on. It isn't near the pools, so I'm totally confused. "What's that for?" I ask, pointing to the clear slide.

"Instead of taking the stairs or elevators, you can slide all the way down to disembark for your shore excursions."

I have got to try that!

"You're the winner of the cruise contest, correct?"

"Yep."

The elevator pings, and I follow him down the hallway. When he opens the door to my stateroom, my jaw drops at how beautiful it is. A king-size bed is in one corner, and across from it is a sofa and a full-size dresser. Past the bed is a wall of windows and a sliding door that leads to a private veranda. I step onto the deck and pretend we've already set sail. My entire body vibrates with excitement at how the ocean breeze will feel whipping through my hair.

Someone clears their throat, and when I turn around, I see Deacon walking around our quarters with no shirt, just a pair of board shorts, and a toothbrush hanging out of his mouth as he taps on his phone.

"Correction. I'm *one* of the winners." I glance over at Deacon and let out a huff. "What are you doing here?"

He holds his hands out in front of him. "Most people call it going on a vacation, but you can call it vacay or whatever you want."

I grit my teeth while I tamp down my anger. The attendant looks from me to Deacon and fidgets with my luggage.

"I really didn't think you'd be so immature as to show up."

He blinks. "Immature? And waste a ticket like this? Not on your life. By the way…" He points at my legs. "What are you wearing?" He snorts. "Come to think of it, what you have on is nothing compared to some of the people on board. I expected Xena, Warrior Princess to pop out at any minute."

Thank goodness he slings on a T-shirt, so I can finally focus on something other than his six-pack. He then pulls out some money from his wallet to tip the man who helped me with my luggage. I catch myself from telling him the tips are included in the cruise, but the attendant doesn't correct him, so neither do I.

Doing my best to not focus on Deacon's physique, I clear my throat and turn my attention back to the attendant, who seems to have been trying to sneak out of the room. "Sir, can you find another stateroom for this… this stowaway?"

Deacon shakes his head. "I'm not a stowaway. I've got my information right here." He flashes his perfect smile as he holds out his boarding pass.

The attendant examines Deacon's paperwork then nods. "I'm sure we didn't overbook this room."

"We won these tickets. *We.* Rub a dub dub." Deacon points from me to himself then back to me. I swat his finger away from my face.

The attendant beams. "Oh, congratulations."

"Yeah, whatever," I say. "Can you find another stateroom for this miscreant to stay in?"

Deacon leans over to the attendant and stage whispers, "She likes to use big words." He cocks his head my way and asks, "Is that the word of the day from Dictionary.com?" Looking back at the attendant, he adds, "She's also a fortune cookie writer."

His eyes grow big. "You will fit right in on this cruise. And I'm sorry, but as odd as it may sound, this ship got booked to capacity at the last minute. Don't forget mandatory check-in is in the Barbados Room, followed by orientation and group photo."

"Can you show her to the boiler room since I got here first? Finders keepers."

The nerve! "What are you? Five?"

"Have a nice cruise," the attendant says as he scoots out of the stateroom.

My shoulders sag as I lug my carry-on to the bed and proceed to unload it. Deacon cocks his head to the side as I pull out a nurse costume and a cheerleader outfit and hang them in the tiny closet.

"Geez. Where did you get those?"

"Etsy."

"I hope you brought some regular clothes too."

With a smirk, I retrieve a little black dress and tons of shorts and blouses for casual, non-role-playing time. When I hold up my bikini, I ask, "Better?"

Deacon scans my body as his Adam's apple bobs up and down and he nods slowly. He slaps his face several times, I guess to bring himself back from wherever his mind went. It's nice to know I can still get to him like that.

In the middle of the bed is a basket filled with fruit, chocolate, and a welcome letter from the cruise director. I read the letter, and the blood drains from my face. While Deacon chuckles, I shake my head. "Oh no."

I shove the letter in Deacon's face and watch as his face mimics my reaction as he reads the newsletter. "On the LARP Boat, you will enter the fantastical world of Belegarth, or as J.R.R. Tolkien calls it, The Great Realms. Although this is not a combat cruise (you will focus on role-playing and storytelling), there will be a boffer section of the ship for specific light-combat activities. You must be registered to participate." He raises his eyebrows. "Ah, so *this* is what they meant by role-playing."

I slink down on the super-soft, comfortable bed. "What is LARP?"

Deacon's body trembles with laughter. "Oh man. What kind of cruise did you pick?"

"Me? We picked it together."

He swishes a finger in front of my face then says, "LARP stands for Live-Action Role Play. Think Dungeons and Dragons but with real people."

I slap my hand over my mouth, not sure whether to laugh and cry. No wonder I kept getting side-eyes on the way to our room. I study the document and point at one section. "What the heck is boffer? That's the second time in ten minutes I've heard that word."

He collapses onto the bed next to me, and the mattress sinks with his weight. "I have no idea, but maybe it'll be tomorrow's word of the day."

He's obviously made it his mission to get under my skin at every turn today. Snatching the letter, I continue reading out loud. "Other activities such as a QR-code-based scavenger hunt, challenges, and quests are open to all cruisers. NonLARPers are welcome on board as typical cruise activities are planned as well."

"How did this happen?"

He pulls up the cruise confirmation information on his phone. "Yeesh. The fine print."

"Unbelievable. It's a good thing I brought this." I unfold the wench costume.

His mouth twitches with suppressed laughter, then he shrugs. "You might even make a few friends, wearing that outfit."

"I am *not* role-playing in that capacity."

He shakes his head. "I don't know about you, but I'm going to have fun on this trip if it's the last thing I do. This ship is so big I can outrun the LARPers, and I bet you and I won't even have to run into each other either." Deacon glances over where the bathroom is. "Except in that tiny, tiny shower."

"Really?"

Deacon bounces on the bed. "The bed's a decent size. I guess they figure we're either going to be on deck or..."

I jump up and cover my ears. "Don't gross me out."

He grabs me around the waist and pulls me onto his lap. His hands splay across the small of my back, and I hate that I don't dislike it. "You didn't always think it was gross. Come on. Let's have some fun. Forget our... issues for a while."

To get his mind from going down a path we don't need to go, I wiggle my hips, digging my pelvic bones into his legs.

"Ow, girl. Stop teasing me."

A single knock comes at our door, then someone slides a note under it.

As I read the letter, I flop back onto the bed. "It's a note about dinner tonight. Looks like we're eating with the captain. Ugh."

"You go and tell the captain the winners can't stand to be in the same room together, but I'd like to stay on this cruise even with all the foam swords and Viking hats. I've never been on a cruise before, so if I need to share a tunic with you, I'll do it."

While I envision all the stuff we'll have to endure, I nibble on a fingernail. The vacation would be so much more fun if he wasn't here to mess it up for me.

He points a finger in front of my face, making me swat it away. "Chris, it's not the end of the world. We can do this."

Of course, he's right. It won't hurt either of us to be cordial to one another while in the presence of other people. As long as no one makes us kiss in public, we should be fine. "Okay. I've done worse. I've done worse with you."

Deacon chuckles. "That's the spirit."

"Maybe we can say the cruise made a mistake and we're really brother and sister."

"We have different names."

As I ponder his comment, an idea pops into my head. "I'll say I'm divorced. That's not a lie."

The laughter falls from his face. "Don't remind me. If it makes you happy, then fine. We'll try that."

That was easier than I'd expected. I thought he was going to be impossible about everything. As he combs his hair in the mirror, I add, "There's one more thing."

With his eyes trained in the mirror, he replies, "I don't like that look you're giving me. What are you thinking?"

With every swipe through his hair, his biceps bulge, and my mind short-circuits. Even if I don't love him anymore, I must admit he has the most perfect physique on the planet. While Elliot has more of a lanky swimmer's physique, Deacon is built like a Greek god. It's only been a few weeks since I saw him last, but his near-perfect body makes me feel like I haven't had anything to drink in months. My heart pounds, and any coherent thoughts I had fizzle away into the salty air.

When I don't answer, he turns to face me. "Chrissy?"

My name snaps me out of my fog. With a blink and a mental slap to my face to remind myself that I do not have any intention of getting back together with him, I clear my throat. "Right. I was just saying..." *What was I saying?* "I remember now. What happens if one of us meets someone?"

He shrugs and sits beside me on the bed again, his shoulder brushing mine. It brings back a host of fond memories that I do not need to be reminded of, so I scoot away from him as he bounces on the bed.

"The bed isn't that big."

"Stay on target."

"So, what's your point?"

I cross my arms over my chest and just spit out what the green monster inside me has already built up in my mind. "I'm pretty certain every single woman on the ship is going to want to get to know you better, if you know what I mean."

Deacon stares at me, his face expressionless. "And here I was trying to play nice."

He stands to remove the remainder of his clothes from his luggage and places the items in a drawer.

To defuse the situation, I add, "Or, it could be me. The point is it could get really awkward. You know... three's a crowd."

He leans against the dresser and folds his arms over his chest, making his biceps bulge. "Contrary to what you believe, I'm not here to hook up. I'm here to have a good time."

With a playful shove, I move him out of the way and open the dresser drawer where he stashed his stuff to see a small first-aid kit and one of those instant cold packs—the physical therapist never leaves home without one. I guess I expected a few foil packets, but I'm a bit relieved I'm not finding anything like that.

"I'm here to have a good time too, and that might mean alone time with someone."

We stare at each other for the longest time, then he opens and closes his mouth before shaking his head. "Fine. If we need private time, we'll leave a sign." He searches around the room then snatches the scarf off my hat. "If this scarf is on the doorknob, it means Do Not Enter. Will that work?"

I was hoping he would grovel and say he's missed me these past few weeks, but it looks like he's doing just fine without me, so I must do my best to pretend I'm doing great, which I'm not. I miss him like crazy, but I feel like one of us should have made the first move to reconcile by now, and since I'm as stubborn as a mule, I can't be the better person and initiate the conversation.

"Okay. It sounds like something you would do in college, but it's the best we can do." I hold my hand out, and he shakes it. Touching him still sends a tingly sensation down my arm like it used to. I didn't expect to still have a reaction to him, so I snatch my hand away from his like I got struck by lightning.

"Good enough."

"You stay out of my way, and I'll stay out of yours."

I give him a playful pop to his jaw with my fist. "It's a deal, brother. Now, let's go to the Barbados room for the 'in case of an emergency' talk. And I've been told it's bad luck if we don't go to the deck to wave at people we don't know as we set sail."

Deacon stares at me for the longest time, then a smirk forms on his face. "Is there a statistic for that?"

"Of course." I throw my hands in the air and bellow, "Boffers, here we come!"

"Just leave my fairy dust alone."

Before I can stop myself, I burst out laughing. Even though we aren't a couple anymore, he's still fun to be around. Maybe this cruise won't be so bad after all.

Chapter Seven

Deacon

It took every ounce of willpower to keep from melting into a puddle when Chrissy pranced into the stateroom, wearing that cute sailor costume that left nothing to the imagination. I wanted to scoop her up and beg for forgiveness, but I've learned my lesson with her. The last thing I need to do is to rush things, no matter how badly I want to. So instead, I brushed my hair for what seemed like an hour. The most I typically do is run my fingers through my hair and go, but I had to do something with my hands to keep from jumping too fast.

We listened to the emergency lecture, with Chrissy taking note of where our lifeboat station is located. I'm sure she's already determined how many minutes we'll need to get from our cabin to that boat, just in case. And as she promised, Chrissy waved to the crowd still at Port Miami like she knew everyone while our ship set sail. She even had me blowing kisses to random people, and I was reminded of how carefree she is. It's nice to know her father hasn't stifled her personality in the weeks since we broke up. That doesn't seem like a long time, but Mr. Parks wouldn't waste a minute to reel her in and make her a stick-in-the-mud.

Not until Port Miami was completely gone from our view would Chrissy leave the railing. She then decided we needed to eat at a pizza grab-n-go restaurant because she was getting 'hangry,' and I know better than to get in the way of food when she gets that way. She insisted on a light lunch, so we'll have room to stuff ourselves tonight at the formal dinner. The entire afternoon was filled with no substantial conversations, barely more than a few *oohs* and *ahhs* from her about every shop we passed.

We hadn't spoken since the day of our breakup. I was hoping I would run into her when I picked up the rest of my stuff from her apartment so that we could discuss things. Seeing that she wasn't around even though it was a time of day she would usually be at the apartment, I took it as a sign she didn't want to talk to me, so I just left a note along with my key. I can't blame her for still being upset, but I'm going to use the cruise as a way to remind her how good we were together and figure out a way to apologize because I really hope I'd jumped to conclusions about her and Elliot. But I don't want to start off our vacation talking about our fight, so I'll play it cool until the opportunity shows itself.

While I sit on the bed, the ship rocks and purrs, almost lulling me to sleep. To stay awake, I consider calling my brother and giving him an update until I remember I haven't purchased an internet package yet, something I need to take care of as soon as possible. So far, Angela's only called me once a day and has stayed sober. She needs to reach me if she gets into a sticky situation. I really do hope she was only kidding about booking a trip on this cruise, but I've been too afraid to bring up the topic for fear of giving her the idea that I want her here.

My eyes close, and if not for the slight rattle of a doorknob turning, I would be conked out. When Chrissy exits the bathroom, all dolled up, I have to sit on my hands to keep from messing up her hair. Her little black dress, which I bought for her birthday, forms perfectly around her gorgeous curves. I'm both surprised and delighted she chose to bring that specific dress. Of all the outfits she has in her walk-in closet at home, she brought the one I gave her. It has to mean something. Or maybe she's just trying to remind me that I messed up.

Chrissy twirls, and her dress flies up, showing off her toned and tanned legs. "Well, how do I look?"

My mouth goes dry, but I recover in a second. "You are..."

She rolls her eyes. "Before you get any ideas, this happens to be my favorite evening dress. It has nothing to do with who gave it to me."

Surrre.

Chrissy pulls her hair through the straightener while I walk out on the balcony. The salty air wafts around me. Taking in a deep breath, I let the wind clear my mind of all things having to do with Chrissy. The slosh of water as the ship slices through the waves below is powerful yet calming. Smelling her peach shampoo, I sense her before she appears by my side. We both stare out at the miles of ocean. She closes her eyes as her chest rises and falls. Her shoulder bumps mine as the ship navigates through the water.

"This is really nice, isn't it?" She opens her eyes but doesn't move.

"Uh huh."

"Even though I don't understand this fantasy mumbo jumbo, I do feel something magical tonight."

Not responding, I cut my eyes to her and grin as she smiles while letting her eyes flutter closed again. I didn't expect to feel the ping of attraction to her when I saw her for the first time, but dang it, I am drawn to her. I need to tread lightly to reconcile with her. If I learned anything from the failed proposal, it was that timing is everything.

She holds her arms out wide then hugs them close to her chest. "I have a good feeling about this cruise."

Let's hope so.

Before I can say, "I have a good feeling about it too because I love you and am so sorry I didn't trust you, and I want to marry you," I clear my throat and simply ask, "Are you ready to go?"

As I lead her out of our cabin, tons of people rush the same way we're headed. It's like feeding time at the trough. I hope most of them are doing the buffet or some other casual dining option, because if we are all in the formal dining room, the ship might tip over. "I'm glad I opted for the flex dining option. Remind me to reserve early dinner tomorrow. I don't care if I'm with the geezers or kiddos. It will be better to fight over chicken nuggets."

"Be careful what you ask for." Her eyes follow another family as they scurry in the same direction as us.

As we descend in the elevator, a tall dude with puffy black pants with a gold stripe down the sides enters. He rams into Chrissy, causing her to miss a step. I catch her around the waist before she careens into him.

When the elevator door opens and we spill out into the hallway, she yells at him, "Rude!"

"Yeah, what she said, Frodo."

With her still clinging to me, we turn a corner, and it's like we've stepped back in time. She glances up at me with a confused expression on her face. We are staring at each other when a foam arrow beans me in the forehead.

"Ouch."

"Sorry," says a girl in a black crop top, black skirt, and green hair as she picks up the arrow from the floor. "Courage! Wisdom! Power!" she yells as she runs off toward a group dressed like her getup.

We enter the dining hall, which has been transformed into a medieval setting, complete with a ring-of-fire photo op station in one corner and a massive fire-breathing dragon in the other. Each table has greenery on it, and the chairs have been covered with burlap to give them a rustic, ancient vibe. The guests mingle like they already know each other, which would explain how they coordinated their outfits. Most wear browns and blacks with leather vests. Some of the women have corsets with long skirts and elf ears. One lady even wears wings. I let out a sigh of relief when I see some guests with typical cruise ship attire.

Chrissy and I stare at each other. I shrug because I've never felt so out of place in my life. "I wonder what we'll eat."

"Pheasant?" she asks with a twitch to her mouth. "Whatever it is, it smells delicious."

"Time to put on your fake smile, little *sister*."

Chrissy opens her mouth wide until she gives me a tooth-baring grin. "Convincing?"

I shrug. "It convinces me."

Her smile fades, making me kick myself for my snide comment. "Try to be nice."

She walks in front of me, her hips swaying with every step, and over her shoulder, I whisper, "By the way, you look very, very beautiful." I could have added four more *very*s, and it wouldn't have been enough to describe her appearance tonight.

"Thank you. So do you."

The captain stands and waves us over. "Ms. Price and Mr. Young-blood. So nice of you to join us tonight."

We all shake hands, and the charade begins.

"Thank you for inviting us. Chrissy and I are excited to be here." It's a good thing he doesn't know me well, because I'm a terrible liar.

As I pull out Chrissy's seat for her, she gapes up at me as if my being a gentleman is an odd occurrence.

The captain takes a sip of his wine. "So, tell me, how is everything?"

Chrissy stares at me to let me take the lead. "Perfect so far. I can't wait until tomorrow to have more time to wander around the ship. We must do everything available."

To catch her off guard, I squeeze her knee, causing her to bump the table.

"Is everything alright?" The captain stares at the both of us.

She nods. "Yes. I'm just eager to eat. I can't decide what to try first."

What is with all these medieval references on the menu? "Look, sis. Something just for you. Turkey legs. Your favorite."

"Yum," she deadpans.

The captain leans over and tells Chrissy, "This cruise is a bit kooky, but you'll get used to it. After tonight, there will be typical dining options."

"Thank goodness," Chrissy mumbles.

A girl in full role-play garb that looks more like one of those skanky Halloween costumes with too much makeup and too little fabric, leaving nothing to the imagination, saunters by. She walks past us and gives me the once-over, which doesn't go unnoticed by Chrissy, who gives me the evil eye. In the direction the scantily clad girl goes, I am certain I see someone that looks all too familiar to me, and I'm not happy about it in the least. The jet-black-and-purple hair can only mean Angela is on the boat, and I am toast. Heat rises, making the collar of my shirt seem suddenly tight. I need to talk to my sister, my real sister, immediately.

"Excuse me. I need to find the men's room."

As soon as I leave, I pull out my phone. *Crap.* No cell service, and I need to talk to Bailey, stat. If Angela is on the same ship as me, I'll never hear the end of it. Chrissy will never believe it's for a good cause.

"Hey there," a voice says from behind me, making me drop my phone. A woman in a too-tight dress walks up to me.

"Uh... hi."

She leans down to pick up my phone, making sure I have full access to her boobs. *Not. Interested.*

She hands me the phone. "I'm Monique. Isn't this the lamest cruise on the planet? I got roped into it by my girlfriend, but she thought we were booked on the clothing-optional cruise. I think I'll rip my hair out if I have to see grown men in costumes the whole time."

"Yeah... it was a shock to me too."

She slinks up to me, and I already feel the need for a shower when she slides a hand through my hair. "Are you here with your... sister?"

"Uh..." Right at that moment, a crew member walks by. I notice his name tag says Zack, and he looks like he would be more comfortable catching a wave than on this ship. I grab him by the arm and say, "Hey, there... this young lady was asking for a personal escort around the ship. I bet you would be the perfect person to do just that." I wink at him and motion with my head toward Monique.

"That's cool."

Monique giggles as he takes her by the hand. *Whew. Dodged a bullet.*

"Where's the best place to get a strong Wi-Fi signal on the ship?" I ask the crew member.

"Go to the internet café. They'll hook you up with a sweet plan. Tell them Zack said to give you the crew promo discount. Don't even try to make regular calls. Not happening while we're at sea. FaceTime or WhatsApp is your best option."

We fist bump as I stumble away. "You are the man."

After running for ten minutes throughout the ship and up three levels, I finally find the internet café and purchase the premium plan because it was the only one that included video calls. I plunk down at a table and connect to my sister. I've never been so happy to see Bailey's face pop up on the screen.

"Bro, have you run a marathon?"

"Houston, we have a problem."

Bailey cocks her head to the side. "What's going on? I thought you were leaving from Miami."

Now, I'm frustrated about both my situation and the fact that Bailey doesn't comprehend my reference. "I'm in the middle of the ocean, and she is on the ship."

"Duh. That's the point. She's supposed to be in your stateroom too." My sister isn't getting my meaning.

"Not her, but *her*. Angela. I didn't really think she would have the balls to come aboard. She mentioned it, but she always says stuff like that, so I hoped she was just kidding, but she is here."

On my phone screen, her jaw drops, and she takes a second to recover. "Oh..."

"I know. I'm kind of freaking out here." I run a hand through my hair as I peer around to see if anyone is overhearing my conversation. The last thing I need right now is for Chrissy to find out about Angela.

She'll think the worst. I know I would. "You remember the role-playing cruise I was telling you about?"

Bailey cringes. "Is it bad?"

"Get this. I am surrounded by... LARPers."

She giggles. "Excuse me?"

"I'm on a freakin' ship full of live-action role-play characters."

"That sounds like fun."

Now is not the time to be sarcastic.

She must comprehend my frustration because she quickly adds, "Maybe you won't even bump into her."

I scan the internet café to see who is overhearing my conversation. The only ones here are two old geezers playing Solitaire. When my gaze lands on Angela sauntering through the door, I whisper, "No chance of that, especially since she just walked in. Crap. Gotta go."

Maybe if I pretend that I don't see her, I can get out of this situation unscathed. I disconnect, and with my head down, I pray she doesn't notice me. No such luck because her perfume consumes me before she arrives, telling me she's nearby.

"Hey, bud," Angela says as she sits on a stool next to me. The purple streaks are a stark contrast to the rest of her shiny black hair. She mentioned she dyed her hair to start fresh with a new appearance, but I just figured she was going red or blond, not quite so vibrant.

I let out a groan as I rub my temples. This day just keeps getting better. "Ange, you are going to drive my blood pressure through the roof. I thought you were kidding about the cruise."

She holds her hands out in defense. "I promise I won't get in your way. I just need you to keep me away from the booze—I clearly didn't think this through." She glances around as people saunter by. "There is alcohol at every turn."

"It's a cruise. Lots of booze. Where did you get the money for the ticket?"

Angela grins wide then sits up tall and pulls her shoulders back. "You are looking at the *Sovereign of the Sea*'s newest yoga instructor."

"Really?"

"Yep." With her hands in a prayer position, she adds, "Namaste. It's perfect. I teach three sessions a day and have the rest of the day off. It's a sweet deal. I wish I'd thought of this ages ago."

"Let's just hope Chrissy doesn't want to take your class."

Angela waves off my comment like it's a nonissue. "If I know Chrissy, she's not going to waste any time on the ship taking a class. She can do that anytime."

Let's hope so. She looks over my shoulder and scrunches her brows together. "Is that..."

Elliot, Chrissy's ex-husband, walks up to our table with a huge bashful grin on his face. Unbelievable. If I didn't think a crew member would arrest me, I would push this jerk overboard.

"Elliot Whitaker. What are you doing here?"

He scoffs. "Did you really think I'd let you go on a cruise with my wife?"

"Ex-wife."

He sits down at a table and motions for me to join him like we're old buds, which couldn't be further from the truth. I have to do several deep, calming breaths to get control of my thoughts before I take the seat across from him. This is not good.

Angela plunks down between us. "Well, this is awkward."

He drums his fingers on the table then says, "I know you and Chrissy are not together anymore, and..." He stares off for a moment then looks me in the eye before clearing his throat. "I still love her."

Angela squeaks. I can't make a sound while my brain processes what's going on. The chatter of the guests all around us evaporates, and in my tunnel vision, I see only Elliot sitting across from me, acting as cool as ice. My head is about to explode. Angela's here. Elliot's here. And I'm about to throw up.

Chapter Eight

Chrissy

As much as I can muster, I make small talk with the captain as Deacon is missing in action, doing who knows what with God knows who. I can't believe he left me to be with that... girl. He left after she smiled at him, and only a minute later, she scooted out of the dining room too. I may be a lot of things, but naive isn't one of them. It's disgusting, and the longer the two of them are gone, the more I change from disappointed to full-blown angry.

"Did you really have to skate on the ice in a duck suit to win cruise tickets?" the captain asks with a twinkle in his eye.

"Yep." On my phone, I pull up the pictures my brother took at the event. "That's me with the snarling face."

The captain throws his head back with a laugh and circulates my phone around the table for all to see. "I hope the cruise is everything you expected."

It's already disappointing because Deacon is acting exactly how I thought he would, playing the field.

Finally, *she* scoots back in, her dress caught in her granny panties. Any other day, I would go into rescue mode and help one of my own, but she's done this to herself.

The foam-finger fighters congregate and speak about things that are foreign to me. I overhear words like *game master*, *snogging*, and *blue sheets*. Some of those terms remind me of when my brother Ty was big into video games. These people are definitely very into their hobby. Two argue over who should be the NPC for the parlour.

"By the way," I tell the captain, "I'm not familiar with the term 'NPC.' Could you explain?"

After a sip of his drink, he wipes his mouth then replies, "All of this is very foreign to me, but after a few of these cruises, I've picked up on some of the lingo. NPC stands for non-playing character. Think of it as someone who makes sure everyone plays by the rules and is not officially in the game."

"Like a referee?" I'm doing my best with sports terms I find familiar.

"Exactly. And 'Parlour' is just a fancy name for the game." He leans in close to me so that only I hear his next words. "But don't call it a game to them. It's a lifestyle."

With a nod, I process his words. I watch as two of the LARPers flit around the room before they settle at a table of people dressed like them. They seem to be really enjoying themselves. Maybe I should lighten up and be more like them.

Deacon bumps my chair as he returns to the table, bringing me back to the conversation at my table. He smooths his hair down as he sits back in his chair. *Ugh.* I can't believe he's already acting like a jerk—and with *her*, of all people. That's not how Deacon usually rolls, so I assume he's doing it to get a rise out of me. When we first met, he waited until he wasn't my physical therapist anymore to ask me out, then it took him three entire dates before he even kissed me, so this is very out of character for him. His face is flushed as he tugs his shirt collar.

The captain holds up his glass for Deacon to clink with his. "I was beginning to think you got food poisoning or something."

I pat Deacon's arm. "Or *something* is more like it."

Deacon's jaw clenches as he paints on a fake smile. I know what his genuine grin looks like, and this is not it.

A waiter stops next to my chair with a platter of the most divine chocolates I have ever seen. My mouth waters just from my examination.

"Would you care for one? We have chocolate-covered strawberries, chocolate croissants, and this one is my favorite." He points at the most decadent piece of cake I have ever seen. "The chocolate volcano cake."

How about the entire platter? "Don't mind if I do." I pick up a praline and one of the slices of cake.

He holds it out to Deacon. "And you, sir?"

Deacon shakes his head. He's such a party pooper. "You shouldn't buy into this cycle of obesity." He points at the platter as he speaks to the captain. "You see, Cap'n, abs are made in the kitchen." He pats his flat stomach.

Even a fake yawn doesn't stop his monologue. I roll my eyes. "Here he goes again. He's in the wellness industry and really takes the fun out of eating."

He squeezes a wedge of lemon and lime into his water glass and takes a sip. "The cycle of obesity starts with Valentines Day. We can't resist those shiny little red heart-shaped boxes. We get to binge and overdo it on Fat Tuesday. Then it's time for the Easter bunny to show up. No one can resist Bunny Big Ears, right?"

Everyone at our table nods. Bunny Big Ears is the best, especially the day after Easter, when he's half price. No matter how much Deacon rants, no one is going to pass that up.

"After that, it's Independence Day, with lots of pie-eating contests. Thank goodness we're left alone for a few months, then bang!" He's on a roll and doesn't even notice that everyone at the table except the captain has lost interest in his monologue and would rather focus on the LARPers.

I let out a sigh and rest my head in my hands, praying he's almost done with his lecture. But he's not.

"Here comes Halloween. Tons of candy. Enough to choke a horse. Then what's next?"

"Thanksgiving," the captain answers in a deadpan voice.

"Yep. Turkey, dressing, and good ole Aunt Cara's pumpkin pie. And a hefty dose of couch potato time to watch football. Then Christmas treats for an entire month. We gain about five pounds during the holidays, start our New Year's resolutions, but then..." He grins, and thank goodness, we've come full circle. "We're back at Valentine's Day again."

Captain leans over to me and asks, "Does he always spoil a party?"

"Always. Ebullient to the end. He doesn't even drink alcohol."

Deacon rests his arm on the back of my chair. "Chrissy, my dear... sister, you need to be on a twelve-step program." He sputters for a moment like he choked on his words then quickly adds, "For chocolate... and your obsession with big words." He guzzles the rest of his water glass.

With that comment, I snatch another dessert off the platter and stuff it in my face. "Much to your chagrin, I don't have a problem. I am completely content in my infatuation."

He chuckles. "Denial." His eyes ping-pong around the room.

Almost choking because I overfilled my mouth, I say, "Really, I'm fine. This is delicious. You really should try one."

"Addicted."

"Guilty, and I'm not ready to come clean from chocolate."

He winks. "Admitting the problem is the first step." His face blanches as he sputters over his words. "What I mean is—"

The captain stands and says, "It's time for the celebration."

"Huh?" Deacon asks, peering over at me.

I shrug, just as confused as he is.

A deejay stands at the front of the dining room with a microphone. "Ladies and gentlemen, let me present to you the winners of the Cruisin' for a Cruise contest from Nashville, Tennessee, Mr. and Mrs. Youngblood."

Deacon and I stare at each other, mouths open. At the same time, we yell, "Wait!" but we aren't heard over the cheers. Even the LARPers are whooping and raising their shields in celebration. Not even me holding up a finger to correct him makes a difference.

Deacon's newest conquest whips her head around so fast that her wig doesn't keep up. She snarls as Deacon slinks down in his chair like he's either embarrassed or trying to hide. I know he doesn't like being in the spotlight, and I'm still shocked I got him on the ice rink for the contest in the first place—and in a duck suit, too.

The deejay laughs. "Come on. It's picture time."

The audience heckles us, the loudest ruckus coming from the Ren Faire crowd. I hold my hand out for Deacon to take. After a huff, he takes it, and together, we walk toward the deejay as the band does a drum roll.

In my ear, Deacon whispers, "Let's just get this over with." His breath leaves a trail of goose bumps down my neck.

As the audience claps and whistles, the deejay scrunches us closer. My face is smashed up against Deacon's body, and his warm breath trickles down my face. His rapid heartbeat pulses in my ear as his chest rises and falls. More *woo-hoo*s and cheers make Deacon's ears turn red.

The announcer laughs and points at us. "Boy, you two are so bashful. Ladies and gentlemen, aren't they cute? Is it your honeymoon?"

Again, before we can answer, cheers blast my eardrums. I stare up at Deacon and can't read his expression. It's a mixture of shock and amusement. As we scoot closer together, he snakes an arm around my waist like he's done a thousand times before. His hand rests on my right hip, and the heat from his touch leaves a tingly impression. I place my hand on his abdomen, and before I know what I'm doing, I rub little circles like I used to do. His stomach tenses, reminding me of those taut muscles just under his dress shirt.

Gah. We paint on smiles, and Deacon kisses my cheek, his familiar scruffy chin tickling my skin. Several women *ooh* and *ahh* us so much that I don't think my ears will ever stop hearing the adorations.

Deacon leans down to my ear and whispers, "So much for the brother idea, huh, Mrs. Youngblood?"

"Miss Granny Panties doesn't look very happy right now."

He scans the crowd, and when he catches her snarl, he waves. "I have no idea what you are talking about."

Through another round of photos, I hiss, "I hope no one caught you doing whatever you were doing with that girl, now that everyone thinks we are married."

"There's nothing to tell."

Through a fake grin, I add, "Think of your poor wife, sitting all alone in our big stateroom, wondering where her sweetie pie has run off to."

He belts out a laugh. "You are good." He motions for me to follow him back to our table. "You will never be a... *poor* little wife."

A moment of hurt slices through my heart with that dig about my father's money. It's always been a bone of contention simmering under the surface. Whereas I never cared how much Deacon made, which is a pretty penny in his own right, I know it bothers him that I come from money and he doesn't. He has a loving family, whereas mine is always worried about one-upping the neighbors. "You will never get past the income gap, will you?"

Deacon sits down and refills his water glass. He downs the contents like he hasn't had anything to drink in days. "Now is not the time."

"It was never the time."

Our tablemates stare at us during our conversation. With another grin that makes his jaw muscles clench, he says, "Later, okay, honey?"

"Fine. I'm very tired after this exquisite meal. I think I'll return to my cabin. Deacon, feel free to hang out and 'do' whatever you want."

He stands and sighs. "I should spend as much time as possible with my wife before she runs off with the credit cards to go shopping when we dock."

"Thanks," I deadpan.

"Anything for you, pookie pie." He accentuates his words with a playful pat on my cheek.

And this is only the first night of our trip. I must stay strong. I can do this. Obviously, a pile of hostility still sits between us, and our time apart has not done anything to simmer his anger. I hoped we could be civil, having to share a cramped space, but apparently, I was wrong.

Chapter Nine

Deacon

Neon lights illuminate the walkway as we leave the dining area. Chrissy's childlike expression is adorable as she points out the green-and-blue streaks of light bouncing off everyone mingling around. A group of people lounge around the pool, watching a chick flick on a big inflatable screen. Without a moon, it's so dark outside that it's hard to tell where the sky ends and the water begins.

The closer we get to our stateroom, the quieter we both get. I scan every corridor to make sure Angela isn't going to be wandering around and surprising us. That's all I need right now because Chrissy has a bee in her bonnet about something. The tension can be cut with a steak knife. Even though the LARP people on the ship are very into their hobby and it was a bit awkward when the voluptuous woman messed up my hair while making a play for me, the most uncomfortable moment was when I had to pretend to be married to Chrissy, especially since, at least on my part, I wish I wasn't acting.

As soon as I open our door, she slips out of her heels and instantly becomes four inches shorter. She moans as she rubs the ball of one foot. "My feet are killing me. I should have found a 'shoes optional' cruise."

I chuckle while Chrissy fumbles around in her drawer as I strip down to my underwear and hang my dress clothes on a hanger again. I could toss them in a corner for all I care. My plan is to be in either swim trunks or casual wear the rest of the trip, so it won't matter if my dress pants get wrinkled.

She slides her hair over her shoulder, exposing her neck. "Could you help me with this?"

With shaky hands, like a prepubescent boy holding a girl's hand for the first time, I brush her neck with my knuckles and see a trail of goose bumps form. Swallowing hard, I slide the zipper down, exposing her back. Nothing is left to the imagination. It would be so easy to slide my hand across her creamy skin to explore her body like the good ole days, but I fear I would probably get smacked across the face if I tried that right now. I do not need to take two giant steps backward. We are only just able to be civil to each other. The last thing I need to do is to assume that we can reconcile.

"Thanks." She breaks my spell as she scrounges around in her dresser drawer with one hand while she holds the unzipped dress in place with the other.

With my head down, I enter the bathroom to wash my face and hope the cold water will cool my emotions. Lost in my thoughts, I jab my toothbrush in my mouth. I'm too wired to sleep, so I snatch a towel off the rack and walk back into the main area, wearing only my underwear. After flopping the towel on the floor, I lie on it and bust out a set of sit-ups. Between sets, I jump up to spit out the toothpaste in the sink then pump out a set of push-ups, anything to keep my mind off my roommate.

Resting, I sit with my back to the bed, watching as Chrissy fumbles around then takes out a nightgown. I snatch the pink nightie from her grip. "Hey, I bought that. I'm surprised you chose that one to bring with you."

First, she wore the black dress I gave her, and now, she's brought the pink nightgown. I sense a theme happening.

She plants a hand on her hip while still holding her dress in place with the other. "It was a gift, and I like it. It's not my fault you have great taste, so give that back."

I jump to my feet and hold the silk nightie high over my head, way out of her reach. "I think I want this back."

She jumps in an attempt to snatch it from my hands but is unsuccessful. "You planning on wearing it? I didn't think pink was your color."

That vision brings a grin to my face. She most certainly wears it better than me. A memory of the last time I saw her wearing it flashes through my mind, and it was amazing. Even as a joke, I think my frame would rip the soft fabric just from trying to get it past my shoulders. Just to get her goat, I reply, "No, but I do have plans for it." I gingerly fold it and slide it into my drawer, knowing good and well no one will ever wear it besides Chrissy.

"Ugh. You disgust me. I cannot believe you would give your new love interest used lingerie, especially when it came from your former girlfriend." She glares at me. "And how you acted tonight... I can't believe you."

"What?" If she saw Angela and is just toying with me until I confess, I may lose my dinner. Angela promised to stay hidden, but she's a bit on the scatterbrained side, so it wouldn't surprise me if she decided to take a stroll, not thinking of who she might encounter.

"You know what I'm talking about. You couldn't keep your paws off little miss..." She does a full body shiver. "Really, Dea. Must you flirt with everyone with two X chromosomes?"

I quirk up an eyebrow at her obvious 'green with envy' attitude. If this means she still cares about me, I can work with it.

"Her name is Monique, and she thinks I'm a great catch." I have no idea what she really thinks of me, and I don't care. But if it gets a rise out of Chrissy, I'll play this game a little longer. Yep, I have reverted back to being a middle-school boy with my stupid 'tug your crush's pigtails' attitude.

Chrissy snorts then pulls out a huge T-shirt and slips it on over her dress. The black dress falls. The shirt says, May the Force Be with Y'all. It's one of my favorites mainly because it hits her right above the knees, and it's sexy as heck on her. And, if I'm keeping score, that's clothing item number three that she brought, purchased by me.

"Why do you take off clothes like that? I've seen you naked more times than I can count."

She steps out of the dress and puts her arms through the T-shirt. "Well, things are different now. We aren't a couple anymore. Besides, you can't handle all of this." She waves a hand down her luscious body. "I've improved with time as opposed to you."

As if she needs any improvement. I bust out a laugh while she pulls out contact lens solution and dumps it into the two little wells.

"I'm sure you've changed sooo much for the better in just a few weeks. The overindulgence with the desserts tonight tells me that you haven't changed much." I add jazz hands for added emphasis.

She stares at me then plucks both contacts out and drops them into the solution. She closes the lids and slides on her wire-rimmed glasses. Some people don't like women in glasses, but she is adorable with hers on, like a sexy librarian fortune cookie writer. "Maybe you have changed... and not for the better, I might add." Apparently, I'm not the only one who has reverted to middle school antics.

With a harrumph, I flop onto the bed and sink into the silky soft comforter. I let out a satisfied moan while I link my hands behind my head.

Chrissy picks up my balled-up socks and throws them at my face. "Who says you get the bed tonight?"

"I called dibs. You should have flopped first."

"Kind of like calling shotgun?"

Winking, I reply, "Exactly."

"Aw, c'mon. No fair." She pouts as she plants her fists on her hips.

I snicker as I toss the socks back on the floor. With reluctance, I rise from the bed and pinch her on the cheek. She shoves my hand away. I fake like I'm going to tickle her, making her guard her sensitive spots. "I'm just trying to aggravate you, which is as easy as always. Want to settle this the old-fashioned way?" I make a fist with one hand and place it in the palm of my other hand. "Rock, paper, scissors?"

She snarls, but by the way her nose twitches, I know she's mulling over her options.

Flexing my biceps, I add, "Would you rather we arm wrestle?"

Chrissy stares at my arm for a moment as an adorable pink flush streaks across her neck. Maybe she's thinking about how I used to hold her in my arms every night. Or she might be remembering how she would use me as a big pillow. She shakes her head, maybe to erase the flashback going through her mind, then sighs.

I know I'm remembering those days.

"Let's do it." An evil grin slides across her face.

"Rock, paper, scissors, shoot," we both say as we smack our palms with our fists. She chooses rock, while I pick paper. I cover her closed fist with my hand, and her eyes flick to mine at the contact. I swallow, hoping it will help me breathe.

"You win."

"Woo-hoo!" I strut around the room, very proud of my fortune.

Her shoulders slump. I guess she thought I would let her win anyway, and a better person would have. She scans the stateroom, and I assume she's trying to figure out where she'll sleep tonight. It's a nice cabin, but it's still cramped quarters with only one bed.

Guilt sweeps over me because my parents raised a gentleman. I should give her the bed without any argument. The right thing to do is to automatically let her sleep on the comfy mattress. We could even share the bed, with her under the covers and me on top, or I would be fine doing the head-to-toe technique, but just as I am about to cave or suggest we could share, she sticks her tongue out at me.

Oh, it's on. "Sweet dreams, sweetheart."

Just to tick her off, I toss her a pillow and a blanket, and she struggles to catch them. She jerks her chin high as she proceeds to make a bed on the sofa then, with a groan, wiggles into the covers to get settled. After she takes off her glasses and places them on the side table, I slide onto my back then turn out the lamp. As I stare at the ceiling with my hands laced behind my head, the rocking of the boat does its magic. I hear nothing except her soft breaths and the sloshing of the ocean outside.

Out of the blue, Chrissy says, "Deacon?"

"Um-hum."

"Did you and... uh... you and that girl at dinner. Did you?"

It would be so easy to lie to her and let her think whatever she wants, but I'm terrible at lying. Plus, my goal here is to win her back, not to push her further away. And besides, she would figure it out eventually then be even more furious at me for not being truthful.

"Of course not. You know me better than that." I run a hand through my hair, remembering the leech messing it up. Bile runs up my throat. "But if I'm being completely honest, I'm pretty sure Zack, one of the deck crew, probably had a fabulous time."

After a long bit of silence, she giggles.

God, I love that laugh.

"Oh, man. You are a dog. You were going to let me think the worst, weren't you?"

"I'm not admitting anything." The darkness hides my wide grin.

After a huge sigh, she asks, "What am I going to do with you?"

I'm certainly not going to answer that question. I swallow hard, hoping my feelings won't be heard. "Get some sleep. I have a feeling we have some serious LARPing to do tomorrow."

She burst out in a fit of laughter. "Oh my gosh. I'll never sleep now, thinking about that."

Don't tease me. "If you're up for it, maybe you can use your creative brain to come up with a clever medieval character name. Priscilla the sea princess has a nice ring to it."

She throws a pillow at me, smacking me right in the face. "Would you... if you don't have any plans tomorrow..." Her words are so tentative and hopeful.

When she doesn't finish her sentence, I speak up. "Since we will be out at sea all day tomorrow, I was thinking about trying body surfing or maybe some rock climbing. You could join me if you want. I promise I won't let you hurt yourself."

Without a single beat of hesitation, she replies, "I'd love to."

I'm glad it's dark in our stateroom because I wouldn't want her to see me punching my fist in the air. I haven't made things worse.

"Good night, Deacon."

After a long, quiet moment, I reply, "Good night, honey."

By the sound of her slow and steady breaths, I can only assume she didn't catch my slip of the tongue. Or maybe she did and doesn't know how to respond. I hope I didn't make things worse, and I can't wait for tomorrow. Operation Win Chrissy Back is in full swing.

Chapter Ten

Chrissy

Day Two of the Cruise

Light pours in through the sliding glass door because we forgot to close the curtains last night. A slash of bright sunlight streaks across my face as the ship hums below me. I pry one eye open and roll over, and I fall off the sofa with an "oof." The couch was way more comfortable than I expected, and I slept like the dead.

With one hand, I help myself off the floor while I slide my other hand over the table in search of my glasses. Everything comes back to me: the cruise, LARPers, the dinner, Deacon. It's quiet in here, and the bed is nothing but a set of crumpled sheets. Never in all the time I've known Deacon has he ever made the bed.

"Turned into an early riser, huh?" I ask myself out loud. I guess Deacon was just teasing me about spending the day together. I shouldn't be disappointed, but I am. At least I have the room to myself to decide what I want to do today.

After a big stretch, I fling the sliding glass door open to welcome the new day. The sun shines brightly as the wind whips my hair around my face. For a long, quiet moment, I stand there on the veranda, eyes closed, embracing the morning. It's going to be a beautiful day at sea.

Ready to face the day, I return to my stateroom. Next to my contact lens case, I notice a note in Deacon's chicken-scratch handwriting. "Your favorite omelet awaits you at the Seaside Bistro. DY."

I bite my lip, thinking of how sweet he is. He used to always leave me little notes like this. Sometimes, I would find a cute message tucked inside my purse or in my pocket, and almost every day, I got a charming text message from him like "I am so lucky to have you in my life" or "I love you more than air." I miss his little affirmations more than I realized.

Dressed in my new hot-pink bikini, matching sarong, and huge straw hat, I saunter toward the promenade deck. My stomach rumbles in anticipation of my goat cheese, bacon, and spinach omelet.

After two stops to scan the You Are Here maps, I finally find the restaurant Deacon mentioned in his note. He's sitting at a table with his head in his hands, obviously deep in his thoughts. Two plates full of food sit untouched on the table.

"Sorry I'm late."

He snaps his head up, and his jaw drops in an approving expression. "Wow." He points at me. "Pink is definitely your color."

His compliment wraps me like a warm blanket. I slip into the chair next to him and *fwop* out my linen napkin. "Thanks for waiting on me."

He nods as he dives into his food. "I feel like getting out of my comfort zone today."

Midbite, I stop. "LARPing?"

That sexy chuckle of his rumbles through his chest as he shakes his head. "Not *that* far out of the comfort zone."

Teasing, I give him a one-shoulder shrug. "I don't know. It sounds kind of fun, if you ask me."

"Most of the guests are in full LARP mode already." He points toward the far end of the boat. "There are so many people on that part of the deck, I'm afraid we'll flip over."

My heart sinks into my stomach with dread. I sit up abruptly. "Really? I googled that since 2005, there have been almost five hundred cruise ship accidents. Do you think we're in danger?"

"Naw. Just joshing. I should know better than to put that thought into your head. I was thinking we could try out the surf machine, like I mentioned last night."

While I mull over his suggestion, I watch his face. He looks like a puppy waiting for a treat because he's been a good boy. "Let's start with something more on the milder side, like the waterslide, and build up to surfing."

His eyes twinkle. "Deal."

We finish our meal in a comfortable silence, like we've done many times before. If I didn't know better, I would think we were still a couple, still madly in love.

"Ready?"

My mind goes back to all the Saturdays we spent together, running errands, having picnics, or just spending time on the couch, pretending to watch some random show on Netflix. It never mattered what we were doing as long as we were together. I really miss those days.

When I don't answer, he snaps his fingers under my nose.

I jump, realizing I zoned out. "Yes. Let's have some fun."

We meander down the promenade deck to the sports deck until we find a massive waterslide that lurches off the side of the ship before tossing us into a pool of water. I backpedal, bumping into Deacon as I point a shaking hand at the beast of a ride.

"That... I can't."

Behind me, he places his hands on my waist. In my ear, he says in a soft, low voice, "I won't let anything happen to you." His scruff tickles my ear as my heart thumps out of my chest. Of course, he would never put me in danger. As much as I should despise him, I can't.

"Any chance there's a lazy river?"

"Maybe a not-so-lazy ocean." He laughs at his nonjoke.

After taking a few calming breaths and ridding my brain of all sorts of statistics on how this is a terrible idea, I reply, "Let's do it."

We climb the stairs while I regret each step. When we get to the top, the staff member hands me an inner tube then gives Deacon one as well. My lungs stop working.

"I can't. I... not by myself." I shove the tube back into the worker's hands and with a trembling lip tell Deacon, "I changed my mind. This is way higher than I was expecting, and I think I'm going to throw up just thinking what it would do to our bodies if we fell from this height into the ocean." I can't stop rambling at this point because while doing my research for the cruise, I came across too many articles about people dying from falling off cruise ships, not from drowning, but from the height.

Deacon stares at the worker, who looks like he's a college kid just trying to make a few bucks during the summer. "Can you bend the rules this one time?"

The poor guy's shoulders slump. "Fine. You can ride together this one time, but don't ask again."

There will not be a second time.

They shake hands, and Deacon settles into the hole of the tube and motions for me to sit on him. Stiff as a brick, I descend on him. He pulls me backward onto his chest. "You have to lie back, or you'll hit your head."

After I run through all the different ways of dying on this ship, I do as Deacon instructs and hold onto the tube like my life depends on it. He grips the tube with one hand and wraps the other arm around my waist. The conveyor belt moves us closer to the ledge.

"No turning back now," he says in my ear with a hint of humor.

"Famous last words."

We slip down with a whoosh into a tunnel of flashing lights. My squeals echo off the tube as we fly through. We exit the tunnel and swing out over the side of the ship, still encased in the slide, but the cylinder we're sliding through is now clear, and I can see exactly how high we are. I scream bloody murder. After two quick turns and a massive bump that almost knocks us off the tube, we're spat out into a calm swimming pool

The splash at the end covers us with cold, refreshing water. I throw my hands in the air as we stand up. He high fives me and has a "Well?" expression on his face.

"That was awesome. Can we do it again?"

Deacon throws his head back with a hearty laugh. "That's a complete one-eighty from a minute ago. I've created a monster."

We hit the Drain Pipe slide four more times before we lounge on deck. The sun warms our weary bodies, and I soak in the rays and in Deacon's company. I can't wipe the grin off my face, even though my leg muscles are screaming from all the steps I climbed in the last hour.

We sip on orange juice and snack on strawberries as we laugh like an old married couple. Suddenly, Deacon's smile falls. He takes my hand and escorts me away from the pool area.

"What are you doing?" I look around to see if we are about to be in the middle of a LARP fight.

He jerks his head from side to side, peering around the corner as we leave the comfort of the lounge area. "Time to learn how to surf."

"What's the hurry? I was enjoying some down time."

"You'll enjoy this even more." Deacon comes to a screeching halt at the bottom of the Flowrider. The rectangular pool with water rushing up the incline may be more than I can handle. An overweight man wobbles a few times as he attempts to surf. Suddenly, the board goes one way, and his body slips another way with a thud. He stops trying to right himself and slides to the bottom then crawls out of the ankle-deep pool of water.

With a shaking hand, I point at the rushing water. "If I break a bone..."

"You won't. I promise."

And as expected, I trust him. Before every physical therapy session, he would tell me to trust him. I knew the exercises he assisted me with would be uncomfortable and sometimes painful, but the outcome would be worth it. He never let me down, and I know he wouldn't put me in danger now.

We get in line, and he rests his hands on my shoulders, drawing tiny circles on my skin with his thumbs. His gaze keeps darting around the open deck area.

"What are you doing?" I ask.

"Nothing." His screechy voice is not convincing.

While we wait in line, I watch the other guests as they attempt to surf, hoping to learn something. The good ones tend to start out on their stomachs, and when they get to the top of the ride, they kneel. Some rise to their feet—that's not happening. When it's our turn, Deacon and I walk into the rushing water while the worker explains what to do. Deacon doesn't waste a second as he jumps onto his board. He rushes down then gets pushed back up by the force of the water. He puts a hand in the rushing water, which makes him spin. His grin couldn't get any bigger.

I slowly lie down on my board, and the water pushes me forward before I can balance. With one bump into the wall, I slide to the other side then lose my board and glide down to the bottom right at Deacon's feet. He holds out a hand to help me stand.

"That was fun. Let's do it again." Deacon looks ten years younger with his youthful enthusiasm. If I didn't know better, I would think he wasn't any older than the guy that let us ride down the tube together.

I double over laughing, but he tugs me toward the line, and we do it again and again until I feel my entire body will be black and blue tomorrow. This is the best kind of tired.

Hobbling back to our stateroom, I collapse on the couch with a moan. He acts like he's going to touch my leg, but I put up a hand in a defensive stance. "If you touch me, I may cry. This is all your fault."

He points at himself. "Me? You could have taken your paperback to the pool and zonked out there all day, but you chose to hang with me."

"How did you know how to surf?"

"YouTube videos."

He enters the bathroom, and when he returns, he's changed into a bright-green T-shirt and khaki shorts, then he walks toward the door.

"Where are you going?"

He turns to face me. His facial expression is hard to read. It's a cross between anger and frustration. After a quiet moment of nonverbal argument with himself, he says, "I have some things I need to take care of."

"Well, don't let Monique spend our cruise award money."

Without missing a beat, he replies, "You know how I am with money."

That's an understatement. I chuckle. "That means you'll spend a full buck seventy-five on her. Boy, is she in for a shock." I regret my comment the moment I say it. After I let out a breath, I put on a fake smile. "Have fun, but could you bring me back something to eat? I really don't want to move out of this position if I don't have to."

He lets out a wicked laugh then shakes his head. "If it crosses my mind." He closes the door with more force than necessary while I put a pillow over my face and groan out my frustration. We had such a fun day together that I almost forgot we weren't a couple anymore. But now, I feel like he's hiding something from me. I could follow him, but I don't think I want that badly to know what he's up to.

I retrieve my phone to FaceTime April. Maybe she'll have some insight. She appears on the phone, wearing her nursing uniform.

"I'm so sorry," I say. "I forgot it's a workday for you."

"That's okay. I'm on a break. You look like you've been soaking up the rays today. Having fun?"

"Today has been a blast." I fill her in on what happened last night at dinner and my morning with Deacon, up to the point where he just left abruptly.

"That's odd. Maybe he just needed a moment to himself."

"It's just very weird, sharing this small space with him. It shouldn't be, but things are different." I nibble on a fingernail as I try to find the right words to describe how I'm feeling.

"Are you hoping he still has feelings for you?" When I don't answer, her confused expression turns into a huge grin. "Oh my gosh. You are."

"That's ridiculous. Our time has come and gone."

She rolls her eyes. "I don't believe that for one second. So why are you sulking in your cabin instead of going out on that fabulous ship and meeting people? You're single, so mingle. Hey, I give you permission to use that in a fortune cookie."

Now, I'm the one rolling my eyes. "I'm not out there because my legs are so sore I don't think I can move off this couch."

She looks at the clock behind herself and says, "I have to get back to work. Keep me posted. And even if it isn't a guy, get out there and talk to humans. Find a fairy godmother who will grant you three wishes."

"Did you know it was a LARP cruise?"

April cringes and nods. "When you showed me the details, I figured you knew."

"Well, I didn't. Thanks for nothing."

"My Aunt Lucky is into trying new things. I told her about it, so it wouldn't surprise me if you bump into her. She's impulsive like that and has more money than she knows what to do with."

"There are six thousand people on this ship, so it's statistically impossible to just randomly run into her."

"I really have to go. Talk to you soon."

I disconnect the call and close my eyes. A little nap is exactly what I need right now.

Chapter Eleven

Deacon

If my brother was here, he would kick me in the balls. My sister would tell me to stop playing mind games with Chrissy and get back with her. Instead, I do the stupidest thing ever: I meet up with Angela. I feel like I have to keep one step ahead of her or she'll pop out from around the corner, and everything will blow up in my face. It probably will anyway, but if I can delay it as long as possible, I will.

Angela is standing on the lido deck, tapping her high-heeled toe as her fingers fly across her phone screen. When she sees me approach, she throws her hands in the air. I'm already regretting this decision.

"Where in the world have you been? I've been trying to reach you by WhatsApp."

"You know where I've been. I saw you twice on the pool deck. I can't believe Chrissy didn't, though."

She grimaces, but by the faint smile, I know she's not completely apologetic. "I'm so sorry, but this ship is so amazing, and after my yoga sesh, I had to walk around a bit. I'm getting stir crazy in my cabin." With a pitiful whine, she adds, "It's sooo tiny."

"Even the bigger staterooms are pretty small."

Her eyes grow big, like her grin. "Yours is huge, isn't it?" When I don't answer, she adds, "Can I see it?"

After I pick my jaw off the floor from surprise, I sputter, "You are out of your mind."

She glances around. "Where is Chrissy, anyway?"

"In our stateroom, and I hope she's asleep. And for the record, I'd like to take a nap as well." I peer around, hoping that Chrissy didn't decide to follow me. She's not the type to snoop, but she might've taken it upon herself to get a snack.

"Good. Let's do some shopping." She takes me by the arm, but I don't budge. "Oh, come on. Live a little."

"No. What's wrong with you?"

Her gaze gets all steely eyed, and I've seen that look too many times. She has her mind made up, and no amount of encouraging her to go back to her cabin will work. "Relax."

Against my better judgement, Angela leads me to the section of the ship where all the retail shops are, and I have a sinking feeling in the pit of my stomach. Any minute now, Chrissy is going to pop out in front of us and yell, "Ah ha! Caught ya," and I will never be able to explain this away. *Funny thing happened when I went for a stroll. What are the odds that Angela booked the exact same cruise?*

Chrissy would never believe the truth. I know I wouldn't if the tables were turned.

She hustles into Pandora and bounces up and down. "I've thought about this ever since you told me about your cruise. Chrissy has a Pandora bracelet, right?"

"I have no idea what that is."

She rolls her eyes and holds out her hand. "Let me see your phone."

"No."

"Give it." She motions with her fingers for me to hand it over.

Whipped, I give it to her.

She scrolls through the pictures on my phone, and when she gets to one specific pic, she says, "Yep. Told ya."

"How do you know that's a Pandora bracelet on Chrissy's wrist?"

"Trust me."

She spins around and takes in the display cases until she finds the item she's in search of. She claps quickly. "Yay. They have it."

The clerk in the store, who appears bored to tears, says, "It's a fan favorite." He pulls it out for her to examine.

She takes a magnifying glass from her bag and examines the details. "This one has a defect on the side. Do you have another one?"

Without replying, he pulls out another one. After inspecting it, she nods. "This is the one. We'll take it."

We?

"His girlfriend is going to love it."

The store clerk couldn't look more uninterested. "If you say so. My shift ends in thirty minutes, and that's all I care about."

I pull out my wallet and ask, "How much?"

Angela gasps. "You don't ask how much it costs. The finer things in life cannot be measured by a dollar amount."

Says no middle-class person ever. I stare at the clerk.

He says, "This one is seventy-five dollars."

My eyes bug out of my sockets. "What?" That charm isn't any bigger than my pinkie fingernail.

Angela's face brightens. "Oh my gosh, it's on sale. I promise she'll love it."

Now I know how a cornered animal feels like. Chrissy never did this to me. She knew I was a stickler for saving money and never made me feel bad for not buying her extravagant presents.

Through gritted teeth I say, "Fine," as I snatch my wallet out of my pocket.

Maybe Angela is on to something. If I show Chrissy I was thinking of her and chose a "spontaneous" gift that would commemorate our cruise, it could win me some bonus points.

We meander down the walkway, the neon lights dancing across us as I keep my head down for fear of seeing Chrissy.

"How are you doing? You're practically surrounded by alcohol."

Angela shrugs. "I consider it trial by fire. I know for a fact if I was home surrounded by friends, I would have caved by now, so I'm glad I'm here."

At least she understands one of the hard realities of getting sober when most of your friends aren't. To be your own best friend, you sometimes have to sever ties with bad influences. That's one thing I learned early on. I had to walk away from some really good friends because "old friends, old habits."

We walk in silence and watch some LARPers fussing over the authenticity of their garb.

"I'm glad you're sober. Really, I am. I just don't want Chrissy to get the wrong idea. And I hope you don't get the wrong idea either. It's over between us. You have to know that, right? I'm in love with Chrissy."

"I know, and I totally support that. But... it appears I'm not the one you need to worry about." She motions with her head to where Elliot is standing, chatting it up with some girl at a kiosk.

He stands out like a sore thumb with his perfectly pressed slacks and dress shoes while the woman, wearing a tight miniskirt, flips her hair over her shoulder and throws her head back with a laugh. That's totally fake because I don't think Elliot could be funny if he tried. When his gaze lands on me, he tips his glass at me. I'm sure that isn't water. He gives me a smug smile. After one last look toward his chatty friend, he heads our way. The slight sway in his gait is due to more than just the rocking of the ship.

"Whitaker. I'd like to say, 'Nice to see you,' but I don't like to lie."

"Hello, Youngblood. Hi, Angela."

She nods, but I don't miss the way she drinks in his appearance. Angela is free to lust over anyone she wants, but if she wants to stay sober, she should steer clear of him.

"Where's Chris?" he asks.

Think fast. "She's resting. I... wore her out earlier today."

He flinches but recovers quickly. He doesn't have to know her exhaustion is due to water sports and not hooking up. That's my little secret.

"Are you and Chrissy back together?"

Do I want to be back together? Yes. Are we? Not yet. "We're getting there, so I would appreciate it if you would stay way over there in the friend zone."

He chuckles as Angela shifts from one foot to the other. "Dude, I only want what's best for Chris. Always have."

"Is that why you're here? To do what's *best* for her?"

I take a step closer. The testosterone we emit can be smelled a mile away. I hate that I let him get a rise out of me, but I've been decent around him up until now, and that didn't turn out the way I envisioned.

Angela squeezes my arm, but I shake it off.

Elliot steps toward me too. He's taller than me, but I outweigh him by thirty pounds of solid muscle. "Dea, you are literally standing here with your ex, and you have the nerve to lecture me about what's best for *my* ex? That's rich."

"He's got a point," Angela mumbles.

She snaps her mouth shut when I glare at her. I did not invite her, so she does not need to interject herself into this conversation.

"That's different. I'm not here to get back with Angela. She's here because... never mind." I stand taller and add, "If you want Chrissy back, why haven't you told her you're on the cruise? Why are you lurking around, flirting with some random woman?"

He blinks a few times, then his shoulders slump. "Because I'm a coward. She's never given me one iota of evidence that she wants to reconcile with me, but I can't let this opportunity pass me by. It's a romantic cruise." Elliot watches two LARPers prance by dressed as fairies. "Correction, it's a very, very strange cruise."

Even if I don't want him to think he's funny, I chuckle because that's an accurate statement.

In a soft tone, he adds, "I may crash and burn, but I must try."

I almost feel sorry for the guy because I know how he feels. He glances down at his feet then back at me. "I have to try."

"Why didn't you swoop in and be her knight in shining armor when we broke up?"

He shakes his head one slow, methodical time. "Timing is everything with her. You should know that by now."

His statement hits me like a knife to the chest. My proposal was the perfect example of bad timing, and because of that and Elliot's words, I have to take it slow with Chrissy and not mess up any chances of reconciling with her. And I'm certainly not going to sit back and let him take her away from me. Not if I can help it.

Backing away, I say, "I'm not telling her you're here, and I'm certainly not going to put a sock on the doorknob so you can get your chance."

Elliot cocks his head to the side, which makes him sway enough that he holds a hand out to steady himself. "I have no idea what you're talking about."

"Nothing. Just please don't spill the beans about Angela being here. It's a very innocent and legitimate reason."

Angela takes Elliot by the arm. "Will you walk me back to my stateroom?"

He appears dumbfounded but tags along as Angela leads him away. She mouths to me, "Go," then shoos me with her hand.

After I wander around the ship and watch a rather entertaining LARP session, I decide to head back to my stateroom, but not before I pick up some food from the grab-and-go restaurant. When I open the door, Chrissy is fast asleep on top of the covers. Slight snores are coming out of her partially open mouth, and tea bags cover her eyes, which causes a smile to form on my face. On instinct, I cover her up with a light blanket then lean in to brush her hair away from her face.

She's so beautiful, even with drool collected in one corner of her mouth.

Before I make the mistake of kissing her cheek, I jerk away and place the to-go box on the table and sit on the sofa, which still has the crumpled bed linens Chrissy used last night. I lean back on the sofa and watch her sleep. Her chest slowly rises and falls in a calm rhythm. To clear my head, I pull my phone out of my pocket and log in to the internet to update my family on how it's going on this trip from hell.

Chrissy rolls over and moans, and the tea bags fall to the floor. "Hey." Her voice is dry and croaky.

With a small nod, I continue to type out my message.

"Say hello to your mother for me."

She knows me so well. I smile as I type some more then rest my phone on the table. "Sorry. You know how I am when I'm in the zone."

She grins and yawns so big that I can see her tonsils, which makes me laugh.

"What?"

"I was just remembering what you looked like, wiping out on the Flowrider."

"Ugh. I still feel it." Chrissy rubs her shoulder, but a tiny grin slides across her face, so I know she doesn't regret our time together.

"And your screams the first time on the slide... They're still ringing in my ears." I cup my ear with my hand as though trying to listen to something. "That poor dude working the slide will never be able to hear again."

She fakes like she's going to throw a pillow at me. "I'll have you know my entire life flashed before my eyes."

I wink. "Fun, wasn't it?"

"Yep."

I love how she pops her *p* with excitement. I love how this feels so natural and easy, like it used to be.

She turns her head toward the box of food, and her nose goes crazy like a bloodhound's. "Is that for me?"

"Naw. It's for the maid."

She begs like a puppy. "Please! I'm so hungry. All I've had to eat is an omelet."

"And you wouldn't have had that if it weren't for me."

She rolls her eyes. I tap my finger to my chin as though I cannot decide if I should give it to her.

"Fine." I toss her the box.

She barely catches it.

"Those years of football with your brother have paid off."

She tears into the box and stuffs her face with food. Between bites, she replies, "Did I tell you he's quitting the job with dear ole dad and going back to graduate school?"

I clutch my chest and feign shock. "Ty? What's his idea this time?"

Not stopping her binge-fest, she rolls her eyes, but we both know her brother has tried every career known to man but always ends up back at the family business. "Physical therapy, just like his idol." She waves a hand my way. Ty always had a thousand questions about my career, so I appreciate that my comments made an impact.

That is music to my ears. "Nice. Is he going to my school?"

She takes her time chewing and swallowing, making me wait for a reply. She loves to make me squirm.

"C'mon. Tell me. Tell me your little brother has some common sense."

After one more swallow, a deep breath, and a long, agonizing moment, she says, "Tech."

My jaw drops. I sputter as I scratch my head. "Excuse me? Tech. That's the exact opposite of my school."

She stands up, grimacing as she rubs her thighs. Food is still in her mouth while she mocks my proud papa march. "Yep. Tennessee Tech. Sorry, bud. UT wasn't for him."

With that, I fake a heart attack, clutch my chest, and fall back onto the bed. "You have poisoned the one smart person in your family." I sing a line from Rocky Top to irritate her because UT does have the best school song ever.

She swipes a pillow and whacks me on the head.

"Is that the best you can do?" I grab my own pillow and whop her in the stomach.

With both of us standing on the bed, we have a pillow fight. She squeals when she gets a few good throws in, of course, because I let her. I place my hand on her forehead, keeping her too far away to get any good licks in, but it doesn't prevent her from trying.

"No fair. That's against the rules of our pillow fights."

My last swing makes contact on her stomach, and she lets out an *ooph*. Just when we're having fun, I mess it up by saying, "Rules went out the window when you started seeing your ex-husband again."

Leave it to me to ruin a good, flirty time by bringing up Whitaker. Sometimes, I'm my own worst enemy. We were having fun. The whole day was awesome until I saw his ugly mug, and that soured my mood. But my snide comment is only making her do the exact opposite of what I want. People think I'm such a confident, comfortable-in-my-own-skin kind of guy, but deep down, I'm terribly insecure, especially when it comes to being good enough for Chrissy. Elliot fits her world, and even though her family, Ty especially, has always been welcoming to me, I think they tolerated me until she came to her senses after we broke up.

She drops her pillow along with her jaw. Even through her hair, which shields most of her face, I see her bite her trembling lip.

I want to apologize for my remarks, for everything, but those words won't form in my mouth. Instead, I add insult to injury. "By the way, did you know... Never mind. It doesn't matter." I should tell her he's on this ship, but now is not the time. After the way I just talked to her, the last thing I need to tell her is detailed directions on where to find her ex-husband.

After a long moment of awkward silence, she climbs down from the bed. She throws her sarong around her waist, picks up her beach bag, and quietly leaves without another word. I punch the pillow, but I'd rather punch myself in the face for my comments.

The soft click of the door is what gets me the most. I know I was a jerk, but she didn't give me the pleasure of blowing up at me. Instead, she picked up her stuff and just... left.

My exasperated groan echoes off the walls while I flop back on the bed to stare up at the ceiling. The right thing to do would be to go after her and apologize. My words were mean and unnecessary. But I let her walk out without fixing my mess.

After I give myself a good talking-to, I wander down the hallway in search of Chrissy. I have to apologize right now. I can't let this fester, and I have to tell her I was wrong about jumping to conclusions about Elliot on the day I proposed.

I pass by the shops, and all the ones I thought would catch her eye are closed. She's not in the dining area, so I go toward the pool deck. Maybe she's hanging out there, lost in her thoughts.

I turn a corner and see Elliot sitting at a table alone, reading his phone. He takes a gulp of a drink as his thumbs fly across the screen. I'm not sure where Chrissy is, but at least she's not with *him*. Before he can glance in my direction, I back away. With my shoulders slumped and hands stuffed in my pockets, I slink back to our stateroom, hoping that Chrissy will have returned. When I get there, it's quiet and empty. Chrissy isn't here, and I'm so frustrated with how I acted that I collapse on the bed and stare up at the ceiling. I don't think we'll ever reconcile, and it's all my fault.

Chapter Twelve

Chrissy

The nerve of him telling me which rules we can play by and which ones we ignore. He makes me so angry I could toss him overboard. One minute, he's flirty and fun, and the next, he's all broody again. I wish, for once, I could read his mind. One thing is sure—he's still incredibly insecure when it comes to Elliot, and no amount of reassurance will ever make him get over it.

I grumble so much as I stomp down the hallway that two LARPers smoosh against the wall to give me a wide berth. "You're smart to move out of my way because I'm not in the mood for any foolishness right now."

The girl, dressed in fairy wings, slides her hand into a pouch attached to her belt. She pulls out a handful of glitter and tosses it in the air above me. Shiny purple and green specks cover me.

"What in the world?"

"Magic dust. I feel an enormous amount of negative energy surrounding you. It will help with your massive redness from the sun god. This should help."

I spit out a few pieces that landed in my mouth. "Help with what? Pushing someone off the boat?"

When she shoves her hand into the pouch again, the guy stops her. "Shining Ella, save the contents of your spell packet for the campaign. It's obvious she's a perm."

I gasp as I touch my hair. More glitter flitters around me and lands on my shoulders. "These are natural curls." I point my finger at the Shining Ella person. "Keep your... magic stuff off of me."

Her mouth drops open, and the guy latches onto her arm to lead her away. She mumbles something under her breath.

He tells me, "Don't mind her. She's a button pusher. Sometimes, she forgets people don't believe she's a healer."

"I don't care what she is, and I don't need to be healed."

"Noted."

"Not anymore since I covered you with magic," she says with a knowing smirk.

With a massive huff, I storm to the pool deck and plop down at the poolside bar. To my right is a woman who looks like she's in her forties and apparently thought this was a fifties cruise. She wears bright-pink pedal pushers, a shiny blue top, and a black cinch belt. Her hair is so tall that she could easily be on the set of *Grease*. When she talks, her southern twang wafts over the bar. The older gentleman she's yammering on to appears to have had a few too many shots. She clinks her glass with a blue umbrella against his shot glass.

The bartender wipes the bar with a towel, and without glancing my way, he asks, "What can I get for you, miss?"

I'm not a big drinker, so I don't know fancy drinks. My mother thought it was so tacky that I didn't have a favorite drink. Hers was a cosmopolitan, heavy on the vodka and only a splash of cranberry juice. Her love of alcohol only served to put a wedge between her and her family. At parties, Dad would usually hold the same glass all night, never taking a drink from it, while Mom would routinely get hammered. Ty and I haven't spoken to her since she entered her last stint in rehab, which probably won't take this time either. She typically picks swanky destinations that have resortlike campuses, personal chefs, and massage therapists. Between long walks on the beach and manicures, she might slip in a session or two.

Not being able to think of something cutesy, I blurt out, "Give me a Corona."

If my mother was here, she would be clutching her pearls, the only person who would actually wear pearls on a cruise.

The bartender removes the cap from the bottle, stuffs a slice of lime in it, then hands it to me. I remove the lime and sink my teeth into it, not caring that juice drips down my chin. I'm not here to impress. In fact, maybe this is how LARPers drink their beer. I take a swig of the cold beverage. *Blech.* I'm not a fan of beer, but it will do. Maybe it will bring down my hot temper a few notches.

I point at the man and his shot glass. "And give me whatever he's having."

The bartender nods as he pours liquor into a little glass and slides it in front of me. I hold it up to take a sip. The liquid slips down my throat, opening my sinuses better than any Vicks VapoRub. My eyes water as I stifle a cough.

The man at the end of the bar says, "You're s'pose to chug it." His words slur, so this is obviously not his first shot of the day.

"I don't *chug.*"

The lady with the blue umbrella drink nods. "Yeah, we ladies don't chug. We sip to enjoy it."

The man giggles as he waves to the bartender for yet another round. "After you've had a few of them, you'll chug. It always happens."

The lady sneers at the man. In a serious Southern drawl, she replies, "We don't have a few. We have one. It's not proper to overindulge. Right, sweetie?"

"Yup."

The lady stares at her drink. "Besides, if you're at a bar alone on a cruise ship, and you're drinking too much, people assume you're lonely."

It's very presumptuous of her to think anything about me or anyone else, but her accuracy stings. I'm finding it weird to be surrounded by a sea of people—pun intended—yet to feel isolated. "I'm not lonely. Just needed to have some me time."

The lady grins. "Well, that makes three of us. Cheers. Barkeep, another round for my new buddies. Whoopie!"

The bartender gives us another round of shots. The dude at the end of the bar chugs his. I sip mine real slow-like, if for no other reason than to aggravate him.

"I am not lonely."

He chuckles. "Then you must be mad... You look mad."

Staring at my glass, I reply, "I'm not mad. I'm ticked. Royally ticked."

The lady giggles. "Me too. I thought I was going to be doing the twist the whole time, but now there are these people running around, sprinkling me with fairy dust." She air-quotes her words.

My mouth drops. "Me too. I have a closet full of sexy Halloween costumes."

"My name is Charmaine, and this poor fellow drowning in his sorrows is Fred. We are *not* together, if that's where your mind went. I just met the poor guy." She looks me up and down. "I've seen that look before. What'd he do to you?"

Fred cocks his head to the side then glances at the bartender. "It's always our fault. Why is that?"

The bartender shrugs as he walks to the other end of the bar to take care of another customer while several people splash into the pool.

"He rubs salt in old wounds."

Charmaine looks at Fred and asks, "Why does your type do that crap? We don't do nothin', and you all have to be so mean."

Fred stares at her like she's lost her mind. "What'd I do?"

"Guilt by association. I'm angry at all men right now, so if one is a butthead, they all are." Charmaine looks back at me and nods. She puts her arm around me and gives my shoulders a hug like we're old friends.

Fred chuckles. "Did you say your name is Charmin, like the toilet paper?"

Charmaine steams at him. I back away because, by her red-faced expression, he's about to get an earful. "Char-maine! Every man has to say that, and that is the most asinine comment. Stupid male bathroom humor. Ugh."

Fred loses his smile as he nurses his shot glass.

Charmaine turns back to me. "This cruise isn't what I expected, but I think it's exactly what I need to find myself. I need to focus on me for a change. Right? Now, first step is to figure out our LARPing name."

Fred snorts, earning himself an evil stare from both of us.

She stares off toward the ocean, and I follow her gaze. The sky is dark, and I feel we are a tiny speck bobbing along on this massive body of water. During the day, the view is amazing, with bright sun beaming over the waves, creating colorful sparkles with each movement, but at night, it's so incredibly dark that I can't see a thing past the railing.

"I'm thinking of Starfish or Freesia. What do you think?" Charmaine twirls the tiny umbrella between her thumb and forefinger.

I tap my finger on my chin as I contemplate my choice. "Freesia sounds mysterious. What should mine be?"

Charmaine pulls her phone out and taps like a teenager. "How about Rain?"

I shake my head. "That's too boring."

"Wispa? Calico?"

My smile widens. "I like Calico." In a loud voice, I yell to everyone around, "From this day forward, I shall be known as Calico, the Fortune Maker!"

My proclamation results in some *woo-hoo*s from people at the pool, and I hold up my shot glass for Charmaine to clink it. I point my glass toward Fred and say, "Your name is... Thunder."

Charmain cackles as Fred's face flushes. She pats my hand. "Now, honey, you just tell Freesia what he did."

Right when I was starting to have fun, she had to bring the conversation back to him. "Oooh. He just makes me so mad."

"Sugar, I've been there. But you can't let him get the best of you."

To the bartender, I signal for a glass of water. I've reached my limit, and unlike my mother, I know when to stop. "What do you suggest?"

She gets an evil grin on her face. "Revenge."

"I'm not following you."

Charmaine leans in and gets nose to nose with me. "Honey child, revenge is the sweetest thing."

I stare at all the people around the pool having the time of their lives. Some are hanging out in the hot tub, while others are settling in to watch a movie on the big screen above the pool. I should also be doing that instead of stewing over Deacon's mood swings. Nothing is holding me back from having fun, and if that means making Deacon as miserable as I am, then I'm all for it. Thoughts of what I can do make me all tingly inside.

"It's showtime."

Charmaine claps and squeals. "That's my girl."

After a moment to ponder, I say, "I don't think I have the guts to do it."

She giggles. "Oh, sugar. You have so much to learn." She throws her arms up in the air like she's a twenty-year-old at a concert and adds, "A LARPer said this is her mantra: wisdom, courage, liberty! I like it."

"So do I."

I pay my tab and say my goodbye to my new friend and wander around the ship. On my way back to my stateroom, I stumble across an impromptu skit put on by some LARPers. A girl in a leather vest and a long skirt sings a tale about six beautiful ladies while women dance around her. Six men follow and pair up. Before I know what's happening, I'm clapping along to the music. A very tall man wearing a red steampunk coat with a leather mask dances over to me and takes me by the hand.

"Dance with me." He sounds like he's trying to imitate a British accent but failing miserably.

"I don't think so." I know I just told myself I should be having fun on the ship, but I didn't mean *this* kind of fun.

He doesn't take that as a no and proceeds to show me the steps, which seem made up, but I follow along, and very soon, I get the hang of the dance.

"What's your name?"

"Uh..." Before I can talk myself out of it, I reply, "I'm Calico, the fortune maker."

He grins. "It suits you. I'm Targ, stealer of hearts."

We step to the left then to the right, turn around, clap two times, and repeat the sequence. I'm lost in the medieval music and this mysterious man. I forget all about my anger and frustration with Deacon. At the end of the song, I let out a loud *woo-hoo* as Targ swings me around.

"That was so much fun, Targ." And I mean it. Something about just going with the flow is magical. I really should do that more often.

He bows low and removes his mask, and when he straightens up, the blood drains from my face.

"Elliot?" I screech. No other words can escape my lips. I blink because this must be some fairy-dust mirage and not real. He can't just appear on this ship in the middle of the ocean. It's not possible.

He kisses my hand and winks. "Elliot is dead in the land of Dunagon. It's Targ, remember?"

This is so not how Elliot rolls. I snort with laughter. "What are you doing here?"

He shrugs as he wipes sweat from his brow. "You told me about the cruise, and I thought... I thought you could use a friend on board."

I side-hug him, and he smells like wet wool, which is an unusual aroma coming from him. "Where's your stateroom?"

We exchange information as we walk around the deck. My brain hasn't caught up to the fact that my friend is here. *How sweet is that?*

"Where did you get that costume? If my father could see you now, he would never believe it's you."

"I thought I would be someone else for a few days. Isn't that the point of LARPing? And besides, there's a store that has every costume imaginable two decks below us."

"If you say so."

This is so not what Elliot would do. Seeing him let loose for a bit is actually fun.

"I found out they have some really cool onshore games planned when we dock."

"It's not a game!" yells one of the LARPers passing by. "It's a gathering!"

As my eyes widen, Elliot realizes his mistake. "My bad."

The LARPers dance away from us, and Elliot and I bust out laughing.

"Isn't this the silliest?" He stares down at his costume.

"I don't know." I watch a few other characters chatting it up, really into their hobby, and they don't seem to care if it's silly or if people make fun of them, which must be liberating. "It seems harmless."

"Want to join in on the gathering?" He uses air quotes.

I hadn't considered that one could have lots of fun role playing—as much as it isn't what I imagined. I figured I would be going ashore alone. "I think I'll pass."

"How is Deacon?"

My mood sours with the mention of his name. "He's okay."

"Are you two back together?"

"No." My breath hitches. "I don't know what to think. It's all very weird right now."

He pulls me into a hug. "Maybe things will work out."

When he lets me go, I glance up at him as he stares off. "I hope so."

Elliot winces but recovers quickly. "Forget about the gathering. Want to swim with the dolphins?"

I swipe a tear from my eye. "That actually sounds like fun."

His grin consumes his face as his eyes twinkle. "Excellent. I'll see you on the landing dock at ten o'clock tomorrow morning. Maybe we can do some snorkeling too."

"I love this idea." I hug him again and add, "It's really good to have a friend with me."

"Yeah. Friend." His jaw twitches, but he replaces the tight expression with a warm smile in a flash.

As I leave Elliot, I stop off at the souvenir shop and pick up a few items to make Deacon's life miserable. I don't want to be too mean—just a bit of childish humor. After perusing the aisles, I choose three items that will drive him crazy. When I reach my room, I quietly unlock the door to find Deacon on the bed, snoring like he always does when he's in a deep slumber. He's spread out like a starfish on top of the covers, perfect for my little prank.

From my shopping bag, I pull out a bottle of pink nail polish and start with his toes, painting each one a hideous Pepto Bismol color. At each slight snore from his partially open mouth, I freeze, waiting for him to stir, but he doesn't even move a muscle, so I get braver and make my way to his fingernails. It's a sloppy job, but if I hover over his body too long, I might laugh in his face.

Without even brushing my teeth for fear of waking him, I lather moisturizer on my face then stretch out on the couch for my second night in a row and wait for the fireworks in the morning. I wonder what view I will wake up to—outside our veranda as well as on Deacon's face inside our stateroom.

Chapter Thirteen

I slept like a log last night and am not sure if or when Chrissy came back to the cabin.

Did she spend the night with some random dude?

Did she hook up with Whitaker?

Did some LARPer knock her over the edge of the ship?

Relief washes over me when I hear the shower running. I wonder what the view outside our veranda looks like today. Getting my legs on dry land for a few hours today will be nice. Maybe I can make up for last night's argument by inviting her to go on an excursion with me—that is, if I haven't waited too long. Most cruisers probably booked those things before even embarking on this ship. Leave it to me to not get to do anything fun because I procrastinated.

I stretch my arms in front of me, and that's when I see the Barbie-pink color on my fingers. I screech, but when I look down at my colorful toes, my surprise turns to anger. Chrissy is not going to get away with this.

Without knocking, I enter the bathroom, steam surrounding me. Chrissy is singing "Hit Me with Your Best Shot" at the top of her lungs. I'm sure cats on the Bermuda coast are yowling from her pitchy concert.

I flush the toilet, making Chrissy shriek with the change of water temperature. When I open the shower door, she gasps. Droplets of water rush down her naked body, which still shows tan lines from yesterday.

"What the heck, Deacon?"

She grabs for a towel with one hand and attempts to cover up body parts with the other. I throw it at her because if she doesn't cover up, I may be tempted to join her.

"You act like I've never seen those." But my words don't reflect my thoughts because right now, I'm like a man who's been rambling around in a desert in search of water, and she's the oasis. I forgot what her body does to me.

She quickly wraps up, and I think more steam is coming from her ears than the shower. "What do you want?"

I wiggle my nicely manicured fingers under her nose. "This."

She bats her eyes at me as she tucks the towel around herself. "I have no idea what you're talking about."

Now, I feel like steam is coming out of *my* ears. We play this staring game as I pin her in place with my sneer. "Hand over the nail polish remover."

She wipes the steam from the mirror and checks her reflection. "I don't have any."

"You will have to go wherever you bought... carnation pink—"

"It's Peony Pink, actually. If you don't like the color, you should choose one for yourself. I did debate whether you were more of a bubblegum or an azalea-pink kind of guy. In the end, Peony won out. It matches your skin tone."

With my arms crossed, I watch a bead of water trickling down between her breasts, making me lose my train of thought. She is as beautiful as ever, even with a mascara streak under her left eye. Her nicely defined deltoid muscles make me long for the days when we would share cramped showers together. Nothing is more perfect than Chrissy stepping out of the shower. I shake the thoughts out of my head and get back to the task at hand by cracking a wicked grin.

Out of the corner of her eye, she stops combing her hands through her wet hair to watch me. "What?"

I pat her cheek, making her swat my hand away. "You better have eyes in the back of your head, sweetie." Before she has a chance to reply, I snatch the towel away from her and race out of the bathroom.

Right on my heels, she runs after me. "Give that back to me." When she sees me roll the towel up and rear back to snap her with it, she puts on the brakes. "You wouldn't."

She takes my hesitation as my answer because I would never hurt her, not even if we were playing, then she grabs the T-shirt I left on the floor yesterday and slings it on. It sticks to her wet body in all the right places.

"Fine. You can have it." I fling the towel toward her. When I turn my back to leave, she swats me with it.

"Ow. You better watch it. That hurt."

"Maybe Monique will kiss the boo-boo." She makes kissy noises and punctuates them with a nice eye roll.

She's back on this Monique kick again. I haven't seen her, nor do I want to, but if it gets a rise out of Chrissy, I'll go along with it.

"Good idea. Maybe she'll have some nail polish remover. Thanks for the tip." I wink as I slide on some clothes and storm out of the room.

When I slam the door, I hear her groan in exasperation. Lost in my anger, I fuss at myself all the way to the elevator. A yelp escapes my throat when I notice my elevator companions. Two big, burly dudes dressed like barbarians holding foam swords stare at me like I'm the odd one.

"Lad, want to join us in today's quest? The onshore gathering is going to be like no other."

With my fists balled to hide the nail polish, I reply, "Er, that is a very tempting offer, but I wore myself out yesterday with all the lunging and stabbing." I mimic a sword fight. They glance at each other because I obviously have no idea what I'm talking about.

The elevator door opens, and the two dudes rush out at the same time, getting stuck in the opening. After a few attempts, they pry their bodies out and leave, but not before one of them takes one last glance my way. I'm guessing they want to make sure I'm not following them. I have no problem with that.

I meander around the ship, surrounded by happy people having the time of their lives or lining up to go ashore. Some take the slide to disembark, and watching them swirl down multiple deck levels is entertaining, but I'm not feeling it today. After popping into three shops, looking for nail polish remover, I consider hitting the gym, but I can do that anytime. Besides, I'm so distracted that I would probably drop a dumbbell on my foot. A massage sounds great, but not by myself. I'm not in the mood to have fun on the waterslide, so I go to the bar—at eight in the morning. A man and lady are sitting at each end on barstools, and by the way he's slumped over his shot, it appears he's been there awhile.

The bartender leans over the bar and asks, "What's ya poison?"

In frustration, I bang my head on the bar. "Got any real poison?"

The lady at the end of the bar giggles then hiccups. "Awww. What's the trouble, honey?" She leans into me and pats my hand.

"Nothing. I am having a blast." Sarcasm drips from my words. To the bartender, I say, "I'll have a cup of coffee, please."

The bartender nods and pours a nice, steaming cup of java. His eyes grow big as he points at my nails. "Nice color."

Pretending to admire the manicure, I stare at my hands and reply, "If I was going to do this, I would have picked... chartreuse. What do you think?"

He shrugs. "I don't judge, but that's mild compared to what I've seen in the last few days."

"Got girl problems, sweetie?" The lady asks and sips from her glass.

"Ex-girl problems."

Her eyes get big. She scoots closer while the man buries himself in another shot. I don't like the way she's leaning on me, so I make a micromove to put some distance between us.

"Tell little ole Charmaine all your troubles. I've got lots of experience being the ex."

This is not what I planned on happening when I sank down in this seat. I shake my head as I sip my coffee. "Thanks for the offer, but it's nothing I can't handle."

That familiar perfume wafts over me, and I look up in time to see Angela walking toward the pool with a yoga mat tucked under her arm. Her boobs are barely held back by a sports bra, and her bike shorts leave nothing to the imagination. I shake my head because this day keeps getting worse, and it's not even noon. She saunters past, hopefully on her way to the pool and away from anywhere Chrissy might be.

The man at the end of the bar follows my gaze and whistles then says, "Boy, whoever this girl is, she sure does have a hold on you."

"She's driving me crazy."

"I can see why." The man stares as Angela prances away, encouraging people to join her in a yoga session and, not surprisingly, convincing all the hetero men to follow her like little puppies.

"What? No, not her. I mean… yeah, she's getting on my nerves too, but right now, someone else has slid into the top spot of annoying me." I show him my hand again, making him belt out a chuckle. "Not funny. There's not one single bottle of nail polish remover on this entire ship, so I guess I'm stuck with this until I disembark."

Charmaine rifles through her big bag and pulls out the most wonderful item in the world: acetone nail polish remover.

I punch my fist in the air but quickly hide my hands again. "You are a life saver."

She snatches a few napkins off the counter and proceeds to make the hideous pink paint disappear from each finger. "Tell me what she did, other than a terrible manicure job."

"You should see my toenails."

The bartender drops a glass, making it shatter on the floor.

I sneer his way. "Don't repeat that."

He holds up his hands in surrender. "I've already forgotten."

By the look of his impish grin, I highly doubt he will forget for a long time.

For the next hour, I proceed to let Charmaine in on my topsy-turvy relationship with Chrissy and how we came to share a cabin. She listens without interjecting any suggestions but occasionally stares at me like a psychologist.

"She's getting under my skin."

After she finishes with my last finger, she replies, "Is it because you still love her?"

Her words sink in, and while I ponder them, I consider my options, which are slim to none. "Because I'm stuck on this boat."

"No, you aren't. Leave for the day. Have fun. There's plenty to do. I've been thinking about joining one of those LARP events and have even picked out a fairy name."

"I thought we had a decent time yesterday, then she pulls a stunt like pink nail polish."

Charmaine sips her drink then twirls the umbrella. "Not having a dog in this fight, I feel like I have to take up for this... Chrissy person because it sounds like you started it."

"What did I do?"

She stares at me like I'm the dumbest person on the planet, and it registers that I did, in fact, start this with that little jab about Elliot.

"Okay, fine. I'm the idiot."

Charmaine pats me on the back and says, "That wasn't so hard, was it? Now, tell her that."

The bartender scoffs. "Don't do it, man. There's only one thing to do."

I lean in to hear his advice like I'm in middle school and hoping to get the intel on how to get the popular girl's attention.

"Revenge. It's the sweetest thing."

She snaps her head toward him and tsks. "You are making things worse."

He holds his hands out in defense as he backs away from us. "I'm just saying you might as well have some fun. Apologize later."

With a chuckle, I think about his words. When they sink in, an evil grin spreads over my face. I pop him on the shoulder. "You are a genius."

Like a bolt of lightning hit me, I rush away, but the bartender yells, "Hey!"

I turn around, throw some cash on the bar, then prance away with a new attitude and a total lack of peony pink.

"You're going to regret this," Charmaine warns me.

But that doesn't deter me from doing what I'm sure is the most adolescent prank of them all. I don't know why she feels the need to interject her opinion to defend Chrissy, someone she doesn't even know. It's probably girl power or women sticking together, but whatever it is, I don't care.

Chrissy. It. Is. On.

As I race back to my stateroom, I think about the best way to get back at Chrissy, but she isn't there. Her glasses are resting on the table, which means she has her contacts in. There goes my first idea, switching the left and right contacts in the case. Her eyes have the slightest different prescriptions, enough to make her blink to focus all day. With that lame idea gone, I go in search of her on deck. If I know her, she's filling herself with carbs and caffeine, and I'm in the mood for some myself.

Thank goodness, I need thirty minutes to find the restaurant Chrissy is in because I use the time to talk myself out of seeking payback. Charmaine was the good angel chirping in my ear not to do anything. I hope I run into her again and can tell her I took her advice. My idea of putting food dye in Chrissy's coffee would only make things worse, and if I want to win her back, I just need to play nice. And when I see her seated alone, looking good enough to kiss, all thoughts of pranking her totally evaporate.

Thanks, Charmaine.

Chapter Fourteen

Chrissy

Still riding high from the nail polish incident, I sit at the Beach Comber restaurant to feast on a delicious breakfast buffet. I pile my plate high with pancakes, fresh fruit, and bacon. *Yum.* And the best part is that I don't have Deacon chirping in my ear about the 'cycle of obesity.' There's a time and place for everything, and now is the time to enjoy this scrumptious meal.

Lost in my thoughts, I don't notice Deacon standing next to my table until it's too late. I let out a groan. "Go away."

He stares at the ceiling while his jaw muscles flex. He blows out a breath then sits at my table. "Can we start over? I don't feel like fighting anymore."

"Pfft. You're scheming something, aren't you?"

His mouth drops, and he grasps his chest, showing that the pink nail polish is gone. "I'm honestly hurt by your words. I made a snide comment about you and what's-his-name, and you got me back. We're even. Let's start over and try to have a good morning. I'll stay out of your way, and you stay out of mine." He holds up a hand for me to shake then snaps his fingers. "And to show you I'm a man of my word, I'll get us some coffee while you eat your... healthy meal. How does that sound?" Deacon knows exactly how I like my coffee, and he seems to be sincere.

"Sure. That would be very nice. Thank you."

"I'll be right back."

He turns the corner to where the coffee carafes are lined up, while I take another bite of my meal. A moment later, he returns with two cups of coffee.

After taking a sip from his cup, he hands me mine. "Just like you prefer."

I drum my fingers on the table then decide to take the coffee cup in front of him.

"Wow. Trust issues?" His eyes dance with humor.

With a small shrug, I say, "I'm not taking any chances."

I sniff the cup, letting the aroma of cinnamon dolce latte waft over me. He made both cups the way I like and even added a dollop of whipped cream. After one sip, my eyes roll back in approval.

Yum. "If this is your way to call a truce, then I accept. Do you want to sit?"

He slides into the seat across from me. "I want to be honest with you about something."

This could be anything from "I'm still in love with you" to "I plan to eat lots of carbs today." I find it hard to tell from that solemn expression.

"I'm listening."

He swallows, then his infectious smile takes over his face. "I was going to put something in your coffee."

My eyes narrow. "You little stinker."

Holding his hands out in front of himself, palms facing me, he replies, "But I didn't because I don't want to push you away."

It takes all my strength not to hurl my body over the table to tackle him in a big hug. That would certainly give him false hope of a reconciliation, so I force my butt to stay anchored in my seat. "You're a bigger person than I am."

Deacon throws his head back with a large laugh. "What are your plans for today?"

So, now he asks. Why couldn't he have asked during our pillow fight? Going ashore with him would have been a delight, but he waited too late. "I was going to sit by the pool or do some LARPing—"

He spurts coffee, which makes me giggle.

"But, instead, I've decided to go ashore... with Elliot."

Deacon's eyes bug out of their sockets. "What? How did you...? I mean... he's here?"

"Ha!" I lean over the table and poke him in the chest with my finger. "I knew it." I take a swig of my delicious coffee and add, "Why didn't you tell me he was on this cruise?"

"Why didn't *you* tell *me*?"

What? I gasp and slam my coffee cup on the table. "Do you think I invited him?"

"Did you?"

"Of course not, but at least I have a friend to hang out with."

Deacon leans back in his chair and blows out a breath then mumbles, "Friend."

"I spent all day yesterday with you and had such a great time until you had to let your insecurities get the best of you, which now, I guess I see where that was coming from. You should have told me he was on the ship. I was blindsided."

He scrubs his hands over his face and lets out a groan. "I don't know why I let him get under my skin, but when I saw him here, my mind just went straight—"

"Straight to I'm trying to get back with my ex-husband?" I let out a breath and allow my tone to soften. "Nothing has changed with him. Yeah, it's super odd that he's here, and part of me thinks my father put him up to it just to keep a watchful eye on me."

Deacon shakes his head one slow time as he stares at his coffee cup, like he doesn't believe me. I'm not sure I do either, and that doesn't matter because I'm here to have fun. If Elliot is here, that's on him. He's my friend, and at least I have someone to go on excursions with, especially if Deacon can't get over his insecurities.

I cover his hand with mine, making his eyes flick toward me. "There is nothing going on between me and Elliot. I don't owe you that information, but I just want to make that clear in your brain. He and I are just friends."

"Are you doing the onshore LARPing event?"

With a chuckle, I reply, "Not this time."

His smile fades. "Well, I'll leave it to you and your *friend*."

Head down, he exits the restaurant. I wish I knew what was going on in that head of his. If I were seeing things from his perspective, I guess it would seem rather coincidental that Elliot is here just to be friends. Part of me wants to follow Deacon and tell him I've changed my mind. Together, we could take the slide to disembark the ship and spend the entire day exploring. It's not too late to find some kind of excursion. But then, the other part of me feels like I shouldn't ditch my plans with Elliot. Friends don't do that, so with a heavy sigh, I leave the restaurant to find Elliot at our arranged meeting place.

With my head down, I bump into Charmaine. She's dressed like a fairy, complete with wings and pointy ears. Just as she promised, she's going all in with this themed cruise. "Hey there. What are your plans today? I was thinking about going ashore to do that LARPing thingy and be a boffer." She spins, letting her skirt fan out.

I grin at her words. "I don't have a costume."

"There's a shop two levels down that has the most adorable clothing options."

"Maybe tomorrow. I'm going ashore with Elliot."

She scrunches her brow. "Elliot? I thought you were here with someone else."

"My life is complicated. Elliot is my ex-husband."

Her face changes expression, and she looks like she's eaten paste. "Honey, you don't need that kind of negative energy in your life."

I wave off her concern. Still being friends with the ex-husband is a little unconventional, but I've known him most of my life. It would be like disowning a brother if I never spoke to him again. "It's fine. We're cordial to one another."

"I should not have told you to get revenge on your cabinmate. You make him sound like a sweetie."

"Too late for that. I need to go. Have fun."

"So, is that a firm no for being a boffer?"

"That is a firm no. Not today."

If I hurry, I can still meet Elliot in time. I push my way past the mad dash of LARPers rushing toward the ship's exit. If I get whacked by one more sword, I'm going to scream.

Elliot is standing on the deck, scanning the crowd. He has swim trunks and a white cotton button up and leather sandals, which is the most casual I've seen him in years. When he sees me, his face breaks out in a relieved grin. "I thought you'd changed your mind or, worse, got a better offer."

"Never. Let's have some fun." Ever since he surprised me last night with his presence, I haven't stopped thinking about how much fun we used to have together. We were inseparable before we took the plunge and got married. In hindsight, we should've kept our relationship at the friend level and never let our families push us together. Things snowballed out of control, and before I knew it, I was walking down the aisle. A nugget of doubt was always in the back of my mind, and I tried to act happy, but it's never a good sign when the bride cries on her wedding night.

We disembark at the Royal Naval Dockyard in Bermuda. The breeze whips around us as we pass the taxis and minibuses taking some of the cruise guests to various destinations. Note to self: schedule a tour for tomorrow. I point at the large sign and say, "There it is. Dolphin Quest. That way."

Elliot pays for our admission, and we meet back together at the lagoon, decked out in life jackets. We settle onto the step that leads us to the water's edge along with the other guests, our feet sloshing through the water as the staff explain the history and mission of Dolphin Quest. When a dolphin swims up to me, I throw her—I think it's a her—a fish, and she gobbles it down in one swallow. A giggle bursts up through my throat, and I glance over at Elliot while he feeds her too.

"Her name is Bailey, and she just had a calf last night." Our guide beams with pride at their newest addition.

Nudging Elliot with my shoulder, I say, "I can't wait to tell Deacon there's a dolphin with the same name as his sister."

"Can't wait," he deadpans.

His sarcasm is so thick that I snicker. "I bet he already has a scarf on the door, telling me to stay away."

"Pfft. That's sounds like something a guy in his freshman year of college would do, don't you think?"

The staff allow us to slip into the salty water and float around, letting the dolphins get to know us. Their slippery skin feels so tough yet also delicate, and I suddenly want to be more like Bailey.

Our session ends, and as I dry off, I can't imagine the day getting any better, but when Elliot guides me to a small boat for a snorkeling adventure at Devil's Isle, I squeal so loudly that I'm sure everyone around me goes deaf. The boat takes us away from the dock for what feels like miles, and after only five minutes in the water, a baby sea turtle swims past, through the colorful reef. I could stay like this forever, but after swimming with the dolphins all morning, I'm exhausted, so I swim back to the boat, and while I sip on a cocktail, I watch as Elliot continues to snorkel.

At one point, he surfaces, and when he spots me, he waves. With hair plastered to his face, he looks sixteen again. I wave back as I take another sip of my drink. Seeing him in this relaxed atmosphere, I can almost imagine what life could've been like if we had tried, if I had tried a little harder to make our marriage work. Watching Elliot in such a carefree moment, I have to remind myself that these times are few and far between with him. Our marriage was more like a business arrangement, one that I had to get out of as soon as possible, especially when his true personality would rear its ugly head after he had a few too many drinks. He never hurt me physically, but the control factor got worse with every ounce of alcohol, not to mention the plethora of insults. His words could be downright virulent at times. I shake those thoughts out of my head. We're definitely better as friends. That's been my mantra, and I need to stick to it.

Elliot plops down beside me, wiping the water from his face. "That was awesome."

"I know. Did you see the turtles?"

"Up close and personal. I need to get out of the office more. Thanks for inviting me on this cruise."

"I didn't."

"Potato, potahhto." His one-shoulder shrug is cute.

We sit in silence as the boat rocks us while other guests swim back from their adventures. As the sun sets, we arrive at the dock. When the last slice of sun slips past the horizon, we walk back to our cruise ship.

"Chrissy," Elliot says, breaking the silence. "I had a really great time today."

"Me too. It was fun."

Before I can blink, he leans in and kisses me on the cheek. I did *not* see that coming. My heart is going to pound out of my chest, and my lungs have forgotten how to work.

"Goodnight, sweetheart," he says in a soft tone as soon as we're on the ship again.

He shuffles away, leaving me with a thousand questions. I need to process everything that happened, so before I make my way back to my cabin, I stop to watch the LARPers as they tumble back onto the ship. They are in their element as they ramble on and on about who died three times. Seems like everyone had a good day.

I wonder if Deacon did.

Lost in my thoughts, I don't notice a sock on the door of my stateroom until I'm right on it. My shoulders slump. I guess he did have a good time.

With no agenda, I go back to the pool and sink down into a lounge chair. I pull out my phone and text Deacon.

Me: Nice sock.

Deacon: Not wearing socks.

Me: Don't gross me out. Watch your back.

Deacon: Why? Are you going to paint my butt pink too?

Me: I'm serious. Watch it.

Deacon: Oh, I do.

With a huff and a growl, I stuff my phone into my bag. The pool is mostly empty because a massive role-play event is happening, and I heard one guest tell another that someone punched a guy, hence the interest for all the nonLARPers.

Hunched over with my legs dangling over the side of the pool, I listen as the water laps around my feet. My flip-flops rest next to me, and for the slightest moment, I'm at peace with the way the trip has been so far. I haven't had a chance to wear my sexy nurse costume, but at least I haven't been on edge like I feared. If I could just get over Deacon, maybe we could cohabitate and not try to kill each other. Even though I started it, I need to get even. *Gah.* I cannot decide.

The moonlight reflects on the water, and if I was here with someone I loved, it would be the most romantic spot. Part of me wants to go back to my stateroom, bang on the door, and interrupt whatever he's doing in there. But the other part doesn't want to know. If I caught Deacon with another woman, I might never recover. The image would be seared into my brain for life, so ignorance is bliss.

I go in search of a place to curl up in that isn't too close to the edge of the deck. The last thing I need to do is roll over and fall off the ship. I could easily contact Elliot and crash in his stateroom, but after that kiss on the cheek, he might get the wrong idea. So instead, I will suck it up and sleep on deck or in the hallway under the neon lights. There's a tea lounge that sounds like it might be a quiet place to snooze. If I had Charmaine's number, I would call her to see if I could bunk with her tonight. She seems like someone I could trust. She would probably tell me to storm right into my cabin and force the hussy out, something I don't have the backbone to do.

As I flip through the cruise ship's app on my phone, I notice some space available for the next karaoke session on level five. I'm not going to let Deacon ruin my fun. I reserve my space at the karaoke bar then smooth my hair back. This is exactly what I need.

Two hours later, I'm tired of watching other people take the stage and embarrass themselves, so I put my request in then strut through the pink and purple lights to climb the stage. I belt out "Roar," by Katy Perry. It feels amazing, and no one seems to mind if I'm a little pitchy. Some people dressed in their medieval costumes even cheer me on from the back.

When the song is over, I take a bow and exit, riding high from the thrill of letting all my emotions pour out through the song. I don't care what Deacon is up to. I came on this cruise to have fun, and that's exactly what I'm doing.

Chapter Fifteen

After realizing Chrissy had plans with *him*, I sulk around the ship, which I practically have to myself. Almost everyone is ashore, enjoying Bermuda, which is what I should do, but nothing seems like fun without someone to enjoy it with. And no way on Earth am I going to ask Angela if she wants to do something. I lie around the pool for a while, hit the gym, then grab a meal to eat in my stateroom. By eight o'clock, I give up waiting for Chrissy to come back, so I lie down.

As soon as my head hits the pillow, I'm out like a light. The ship is mostly still since we're staying in port for another night, and the gentle rocking sends me to la-la land faster than a newborn baby with a full tummy.

Laughter in the hallway wakes me up, and I realize a new day has dawned. The sun shines through the sliding glass door, and it looks like it's going to be another picture-perfect day. I sprawl out on the bed, stretching my legs as I think back to yesterday. *She spent the entire day with that... dude. Did they have fun? Where was she all night? Did they run off and elope in Bermuda? Are they going to build a shack on the coastline and have tons of babies?* The last question makes me chuckle because Elliot would never be happy living in anything smaller than a mini mansion.

But, like she said, I waited too late to ask her to accompany me, so that's partially my fault. I wonder if that's a metaphor for my life. My timing is always off with Chrissy. If I haven't totally messed things up, I'm going to fix things with her, starting with a long-overdue apology for everything I've done.

My sister, Bailey, would have a fit if I wasted another full day sulking in my room when I could go ashore and explore. With reluctance and a deep sigh, I rise to get a hot shower. The thought of leaving the ship alone depresses me, but I'll be damned if I ask Angela to go with me. She's getting her vitamin D on deck and recharging with massages between yoga classes. So far, she's checked in a few times but has created no more surprises, and she's managed to stay sober, so good for her.

When the water turns cold, I force myself out of the shower. As I stare at my scruffy face in the mirror, I hear the door open and shut with sizable force. I peek my head out of the bathroom to see Chrissy standing there in wrinkled clothes. Her hair is a frizzy, wind-blown mess.

"Good morning, sexy. I trust you slept well." That's probably the worst opening line ever, but I can't help myself.

She steels her eyes on me, and I shrink back into the bathroom, waiting for the wrath of Priscilla Christine to blow. She has focused her anger in my direction only a handful of times, and it was never pretty.

"I hope you had a fun night in a comfortable bed. Curled up with some floozy, no doubt."

I wipe my face, throw on a T-shirt and shorts, then exit the bathroom. She flops on the couch, looking completely haggard.

I sink down next to her to slip on my Vans. "Actually, now that I think about it, I had a great night. How about you?"

She pops me on the arm.

"Ow!"

"I know that didn't hurt, and you know what kind of night I had. I ended up sleeping on a lounge chair next to the pool. Where did you expect me to sleep? I nearly froze my butt off."

And why is this my problem? I shrug as I rise. "Did you lose your key card?"

Her shoulders slump. "No."

"Why didn't you come in? I was here all night."

She blows out a breath as a flush creeps up her neck. "I just thought…" She runs her fingers through her hair, but they get stuck in a knot halfway.

"Thought what?"

She looks away from me and fidgets with a fingernail. "I don't know."

"What are you talking about?"

"Never mind."

When our eyes meet, I see hurt in her eyes. I have no idea what's upset her, but I know for a fact I haven't done anything this time, so I snatch my phone off the table and send Bailey a quick message, about to break the glass display with my angry typing. "You chose to spend the day and, for all I know, the entire night with Elliot, so don't make me feel bad for anything."

"I did not spend the night with him."

Without glancing up, I focus on the message from my sister. She wants to know if I've begged for Chrissy to take me back. I send her a one-word reply: "Nope."

She picks up a brush to work on her unruly, windswept hair. "How's Angela?" Her quivering voice doesn't cover her bitter sarcasm. She hates my ex-girlfriend more than I despise her ex-husband, and that's saying a lot.

"How should I know?"

Chrissy swings around and doesn't say a word until I look up.

"What?"

"You haven't talked to her?"

"Why would you think that?"

She knows, and she knows I know. Great…

She stares at me then blows out a breath. "Never mind. It's none of my business."

My sister immediately replies, but I don't have the patience to deal with her right now. I stand to move within an inch of Chrissy. Her head is bowed as she fidgets with the hem of her shirt. My instinct is to brush her hair behind her ear, but right before my hand touches her, she jumps up, grabs some clean clothes out of the drawer, and rushes to the bathroom.

Over her shoulder she says, "Today is going to be a beautiful day, and I'm going ashore again." With hesitation in her voice, she adds, "Would you like to... join me?"

I walk to the bathroom. Her hopeful eyes won't let me disappoint her, as if I would. I'm mentally punching my hand in the air in jubilation. *Yes!*

After I stare at the ceiling to delay my response and not seem so eager, I grin. "I would love to. Get dressed."

Her eyes grow wide as her mouth drops. "Really?"

"Yes, but you better get ready fast before I change my mind."

Like a cheerleader, she bounces up and down and into my arms. My arms encircle her waist, and I enjoy the contact.

When she realizes what she's done, she pushes away and clears her throat. "I would love to take the ferry to Hamilton. How does that sound?"

I will do whatever she wants. "That sounds perfect." I'm so proud of myself for sounding so chill when all I want to do is scoop her up and kiss those beautiful lips.

"And then shopping too! We're going shopping! Woo-hoo!" Chrissy boogies around the room and sings the song "Roar" as she decides on an outfit for the day.

She's so cute. I shake my head as I watch her shimmy around the room. It doesn't take much to make her happy, unlike some women I know.

"Settle down, Katy Perry. We'll do anything you want." I only want to do two things today: spend time with my girl and make sure she doesn't think of *him*.

Things haven't been going as planned on this trip, but maybe we can clear the air today and move forward and not backward. Otherwise, I may need to sleep on deck for the rest of the cruise.

In record time, she exits the bathroom shower fresh. Her wet hair sticks to her neck as she towel dries it.

"Let me help."

While she applies makeup, which she doesn't need, I run my fingers through her wet strands, untangling them. With every stroke, I feel my heart being tugged back to her, and I'm tired of fighting it. We should clear the air and start fresh.

Right when I'm about to spill my guts about how sorry I am for doubting her and wanting another chance, she blurts out, "I swam with a dolphin yesterday named Bailey."

The glint in her eye tells me she had a good time. I laugh at the vision of her giggling with the animal swimming around her. "You'll have to tell my sister. She'll get a kick out of it."

When I glance at her reflection in the mirror, I catch her staring at me. Heat flushes my neck and ears. "I think I have all the tangles out. It should be ready for you to do your magic."

She swallows as she nods. Her nimble fingers work through her hair, and within minutes, it's pulled into a French braid.

"I'm guessing you had fun with Elliot." *Real slick, Dea. You were supposed to make her forget him, and here you go bringing up his name.*

Chrissy nods. "It was nice seeing the way he used to be, but..."

"What?" I hope my eagerness doesn't show in my voice.

She works her teeth over her bottom lip before she says, "He kissed me."

I freeze as this punch to the gut settles in. While I was picking stupid, petty fights with her, he didn't waste any time trying to win her back. And he made a big leap in the right direction. I'm not sure if I want to know how she feels about it.

"Where?"

"On the ship when we got back from our excursion."

"I mean... where? On your—"

"It was just a peck on the cheek, and I don't know how to process it, not that it matters anyway. The divorce rate of second marriages is astronomical."

She's going to kick my butt, but I can't help but smile. For once, her stats are coming in handy.

"I want you to be happy, Chris." In the mirror, I watch as she processes my comment.

Her eyes flick to mine. "I probably shouldn't have told you that, but I wanted to be honest with you, and besides, I didn't get the flippy-floppy feeling with that kiss."

My eyebrows raise. "Flippy-floppy?"

She nudges me with her shoulder. "You know what I mean."

When she swings around to face me, I want so badly to give her a kiss, one that won't leave any doubt in her mind about how I feel, but that won't make anything better at this point, so I clear my throat and, with a hint of humor in my voice, ask, "Did you ever get the flippy-floppy feeling with me?"

Chrissy focuses on her nails as she says barely above a whisper, "Every time."

Yes! My sister says that if a girl doesn't get a 'foot pop' when you kiss her, it didn't mean much to her. I guess Chrissy's 'foot pop' is her fluttery feeling.

"We're burning daylight," I say. "Let's go."

If we don't get out of this cabin right now, I might give her those floppy feelings all day long. She doesn't move. I don't move. We stand there, gazing into each other's eyes for the longest time. I slide a hand over her bare arm, and she watches as a trail of goose bumps appears. I tug her closer, but she takes a step backward and tucks a stray hair behind her ear.

Her infectious grin melts all my insecurities. I can't win her back by bad-mouthing Elliot. Obviously, that would only push her toward him. So the only thing that will work is to be myself. If we are meant to be together, we'll work things out.

"Ready?" Her question breaks the spell I'm under.

I can only reply with a nod as I escort her out of our stateroom.

I clear my throat and, in a low voice, say, "I didn't mean what I said yesterday."

"I know. Me either."

"I'm sorry. About a lot of things." I search her face for a reaction. *Is it too little, too late? Will she just put me in her pile of male friends alongside Whitaker?*

"Thank you." Her response is quiet and breathy. She slips an arm through mine, and the air around us already feels lighter. If I can keep my foot out of my mouth, this may be a great day.

Chapter Sixteen

Deacon eyes me with suspicion. "Are you sure you want to do this?"

I stare down at the clear enclosed slide, which swirls down six levels. One by one, guests slip down the length of the tube as a fast track off the ship. "Absolutely. We'll spend all day waiting on an elevator, and this looks like way more fun."

"We could take the stairs."

With a scoff, I add, "Where's the fun in that?"

He shakes his head like he doesn't know what to make of me, but he helps me enter the tube, and we descend in a slow, steady fashion. With each turn, a different level appears, revealing hordes of people meandering around the ship.

At the bottom of the slide, we come to a halt, and an attendant helps me to my feet.

"Can we take the elevator back up and do it again?"

Deacon shakes his head as laughter rumbles through him. "Wasn't it just two days ago when you let out a bloodcurdling scream on the waterslide?"

I hold up a hand to correct him. "Only the first time. I got over my fear after that." *If I could've gotten over my fear of a second failed marriage, this could've been our honeymoon.*

The seagulls welcome us to Bermuda's Kings Wharf berth, and even the LARPers are dressed in casual attire for their day of excursions. Deacon slides on his sunglasses as he looks over the narrow strip of land that will take us to the Royal Navy Dockyard. Even though I was here just yesterday with Elliot, this feels better, different, normal.

While we walk toward an old structure that houses two clocktowers, I peek over at my companion. Deacon looks good enough to eat, with his tight but not too tight green T-shirt that brings out his eyes and khaki shorts that show off his tanned, muscular calves.

As much as I love the cruise, I felt great yesterday with my feet on steady ground, so I'm eager to do it again, and strangely, I'm craving some alone time with Deacon outside our stateroom. That room was getting a bit hot even though the air conditioner was blasting.

He holds my hand as we walk down the North Arm and away from our ship. I'm reminded of how the little displays of affection with Deacon are so special. The hand holding, brushing my hair, our inside jokes, they all mean more than a grand gesture ever could. I know he has some insecurities when it comes to money, but no large bank account can compete with simple acts of kindness, and he has those in spades.

We saunter down the dockyard, away from the ship. Street vendors are all around us, urging us to buy one of their items, and of course, I must check out each one. The fruits smell like heaven, but I know I shouldn't buy any because I wouldn't have anywhere to store them on the plane ride home. Flowers are everywhere, and some varieties I only wish I could grow in my apartment back home. The colors are so vibrant that no one could be grumpy around them. And the hats—I want them all. Deacon is as patient as a saint as I indulge myself at every cart. I don't buy anything yet because I don't want to lug it around all day, but he knows I love to window-shop.

We nestle together as we take the ferry to Hamilton, the capital of Bermuda. Thank goodness, my hair is braided. Otherwise, it would become a tangled mess as we get closer to our destination and our cruise ship gets smaller and smaller in the background.

Deacon convinces me to rent electric bikes to ride down the winding road toward Fort Scaur. Being the nice person he is, we stop along the way to rest and absorb the lush scenery all around. He snaps photos of us against the rich flora. A monarch butterfly lands on my big straw hat, and my eyes grow wide as I slowly point at it.

"Don't move," Deacon instructs me as he snaps another photo while I peer upward in an attempt to see the orange-and-black wings. "Got it right before it flew away."

He shows me the picture, and I snag his phone out of his hand to take a selfie of us in front of an enormous bird of paradise. I've never seen anything so bright orange.

When we arrive at the fort, we absorb all the glory that only a structure this old and this well preserved can hold. As we stand at the edge of the fort, overlooking the panoramic view of the Great Sound of Bermuda, we can see the Royal Naval Dockyard in the distance.

I point out toward the dockyard. "I think that's our ship. It seems so far away."

Deacon stands next to me, and his shoulder brushes mine. "I guess it's like life. Sometimes, it feels like what you need is way out of reach, but put it into perspective, and it's not like that at all."

"How very philosophical of you."

He turns me around and retrieves his phone from his pocket. "Selfie time again."

After several attempts to get the perfect shot, he shows me the screen. With the way we're nestled together, smiling at one another, any outsider would assume we're a happy little couple. It almost convinces me. My emotions are all over the place, and right when I'm about to tell him I want to reconcile, he takes my hand, breaking up my thoughts.

"Do you think we have time to visit the Gibb's Hill Lighthouse and still make the ferry back to the dockyard?"

"Are you just trying to get your steps in while getting to the top?"

His guilty smile says it all.

"On top of that, you'll make me bike there."

He smirks, and when I pop him in the stomach, he says, "Okay, we can catch a ride there instead of cycling."

Music to my ears! I'm so glad he's willing to compromise because if I had to bike all the way to the lighthouse, I would have to gaze at it from the ground. Deacon holds my hand, guiding me as we huff and puff—mostly me—to the top of the tall enclosure. My lungs are on fire when we pop out at the top, so I lean against the iron structure to catch my breath. Deacon is all smiles and doesn't act like he's winded at all.

"My quads are screaming."

"I'll carry you down if I need to."

"Ha ha." I hope my nervousness isn't obvious because I'm within seconds of taking him up on it, and I know he would. "What do we do now that we made it to the top?"

With a content expression on his face, he breathes deeply. "We enjoy the view and the moment."

"I can do that." The view is gorgeous, and I'm beginning to realize no bad scenes exist in Bermuda, especially the view of the attractive man standing next to me.

Several other people pile into the tiny space, squeezing me right up against Deacon's chest.

He slides a hand around my waist as he whispers, "I guess we should go down."

I should take him up on the offer to carry me, but I don't. I almost need an inhaler when I get to the bottom, but he was right. The view was breathtaking and worth every labored breath.

We're both quiet on the ferry ride back. Maybe it's because we're in awe of the beauty all around us, or perhaps it's because we're both exhausted. For me, it's because I don't want to ruin this feeling with words. Other than a big gust of wind that whips my hat into the waves, gone forever, the ride was uneventful. Once our ferry is docked again at Kings Wharf, I notice the Clocktower Mall. *Must. Shop. Now.* My ten minutes of ferry ride has rejuvenated me. I glance at Deacon with a pleading expression, and as always, he obliges.

To our right, I see a dress shop that I cannot pass without checking it out. Pulling Deacon inside, I set out to try on some items. This is probably the last thing he wants to do, but if he doesn't speak up about his wishes, this is what we will do until the time comes to head back to the ship. While he sits on a fluffy chair, surrounded by feminine clothing, I try on different items not of the role-playing variety. I whip open the changing curtain and strut around the store in front of Deacon to get his opinion. He crinkles his nose in disapproval, which I have to agree with. The next is a nautical suit, a striking white jacket with a skirt that hits me midcalf. The jacket has fake ribbons as if I've earned some medals, along with very big shoulder pads. Deacon cringes, and again, I'm glad.

"Wait, I'm not done." I slide back into the changing room to slip on a massive, oversized straw hat. I come out of the room with a ta-da expression. "You know I have to replace the one that I'm sure Flipper is now wearing."

He chuckles. "The hat is a yes, but that suit... not on your life."

A moment later, I exit again with an oversized T-shirt that has I Heart Bermuda on the front, to find Deacon with his chin on his chest, snoozing. I clear my throat, and he jolts awake.

"What did I miss?"

"What do you think of this one?"

"Meh."

"Okay, is this any better?" I whip off the shirt to reveal a very skimpy black bikini. His jaw drops as he nods in approval. I love his reaction, and I can't deny how his expression warms me.

"Hungry?" he asks when I've changed back into my regular clothes and get in line to pay for my hat and bathing suit.

"Famished." *For food and you.*

Spending time with Deacon today has been very amiable and comfortable, like it used to be. We finish each other's sentences and laugh at everything, even if no one else would think it's humorous. We are partners in crime, and I really, really miss that. I miss him.

We stop at the Bone Fish Bar and Grill to have a bite to eat. It's a two-story red-brick structure so close to the water's edge that I can almost reach out and touch our ship. Deacon picks a bistro table outside that overlooks the harbor. A breeze starts blowing, so I double-tie my hat, making sure I don't lose another one. My colorful shopping bags rest at my feet. Deacon was very sweet to carry them for me, because that's the kind of guy he is. Even when he doesn't like me, he's still a perfect gentleman, and he sure doesn't act like he hates me today.

Deacon peruses the menu as though he doesn't already know what he wants to eat. "Abs are made in the kitchen" is his mantra, and it must work because his are rock-solid. To the waiter, he says, "I'll have the Crunchy Spicy Seafood Salad."

I feign shock. "No typical Caesar salad, baked salmon, and steamed vegetables?"

He cracks a grin. "I'm trying new things."

"It's good to see you branch out of your comfort zone." I glance up at the waiter and say, "I think I'll have the fish tacos."

"Oh, that sounds good. Can you switch my order to that?"

Now, my jaw is on the floor. Deacon is never spontaneous with food choices, and he certainly never changes his mind. I like that he's loosening up a bit.

He sips from his water glass as he eyes me with suspicion. "What did I do?"

I give him the slightest shrug. "It's nice to see you be more... open-minded."

"It's just food."

With a knowing glance, I say, "I think there's a metaphor in there somewhere. Maybe I should jot it down for a fortune cookie. Life is like food. Once it's gone, you can't get it back."

Deacon's eyes twinkle. "Or you could write, 'Life is like food. Most of the time, it turns out to be—'"

"I like mine better."

We clink water glasses as we sit in silence for a moment. "That's what I like about you, Chrissy. You're always the glass-is-half-full kind of person. I wish I was more like you."

My grin consumes my face. He'll never know how touching that compliment is. Most people, Elliot included, think I'm a Pollyanna and way too optimistic all the time. That's how I got talked into marrying someone I wasn't in love with. *It'll be fine. I can make it work,* I told myself. And even after my divorce, I had this opinion that I could still be friends with my ex-husband. *It'll be fine. I can make it work.*

Maybe I am too optimistic, but even if I'm wrong sometimes, I still want to see the good in situations, in people. However, I must be real with myself. Sometimes, things are not going to be okay, and some people will let me down. But I can pick myself up and try again, love again. And if Deacon is willing to try new things, even if it's just fish tacos instead of his usual salad, maybe getting married again, this time to the right person, isn't so scary after all.

We sit in silence for a moment until the waiter brings our drinks and crab appetizer.

Thinking of a way to segue into a neutral, nonconfrontational conversation, I ask, "How's work? Have you had any chatty women with ankle injuries lately?" I know he welcomes any opportunity to talk about his profession, and the memory of when Deacon was assigned as my physical therapist was a special day in my life. I was smitten from the first session, and I might have made it seem as though my injury was worse than it was so that I could have an excuse to see him. Thinking he would never ask me out, I made the first move. He said he was waiting until our professional relationship was over before he asked me on a date. If I'd known that, I would have been miraculously healed after day one.

He stops eating then smiles that sexy grin I love so much. "Work has been pretty normal. No women fawning over me." He leans back and stares at the clear blue sky. "I miss those days." That swoonworthy wink tells me he's just kidding.

I ball up my napkin and toss it at him. "You were so clueless. I was practically throwing myself at you, and you were all business all the time. It took every ounce of willpower not to purr every time you touched my ankle. It was pure torture, and I didn't think you felt the electricity zipping between us."

"I felt it." His gaze begins smoldering, and I feel a pull toward him as much today as I did during those physical therapy sessions.

I'm not sure where this conversation is going, but for both of us, it needs to return to playful banter fast, or I may not ever want to leave this island, so I pivot to a completely opposite and mood-killing topic. "How's your mom?"

Deacon smiles so big that I think his face is going to split wide open. His tight-knit family is a far cry from my own, and that was another layer of the relationship that was ripped from me. They took me in as another Youngblood, sharing their love with me like I'd never had with my own family. My brother, Ty, is great, but the parents are too caught up in keeping up with the Joneses to listen to my wants and needs.

"Same ol' mom."

My smile fades as I think of her and how much I miss her. An older couple walk by hand in hand, looking like they've been in love for decades.

"I miss her."

He clears his throat and wipes his mouth with a napkin. "If it makes you feel any better, she asks about you. All. The. Time."

"Really?" My heart swells because she still cares enough about me to ask how I'm doing. My own mother doesn't even do that.

As the waiter stops by with our food, Deacon nods while gulping some water. "Mom drives me crazy, but you know how she can be. Totally harmless. Pushy, yes, but not a mean bone in her body."

"Definitely. She's a gem. I just wish my own mother would ask about me." Admitting that out loud is hard, but Deacon knows my story, and I feel one hundred percent comfortable being honest with him.

He cuts his eyes to me. "Still AWOL?"

"Yeah, but I have a father to make up for things... opens his heart... and wallet. We are a happy, happy bunch." I hope my sarcasm can be heard loud and clear because Deacon has always felt inadequate in the financial department even though his salary is amazing. It's not "old money," thus he never completely felt comfortable with the stodgy men in my father's social circle.

"Why didn't you tell me Elliot was on the ship?" That's a mood killer for the decades, but I have to ask.

He stops eating and clears his throat then shrugs. "I don't know. I guess I thought you already knew."

"Nope, and I would have appreciated a heads-up."

He holds his hands up in defense. "It's not like he texted me weeks ago and said, 'Hey, I heard you broke up with Chrissy, so I'm coming along on the cruise to make your life even more miserable.' I just ran into him on the ship, and let's just say... I have never trusted him with this 'just friends' mumbo jumbo." An eye roll and air quotes emphasize his irritation. "And now that I know he kissed you..."

Guilt washes over me because I should have kept that to myself, at least until I worked it all out in my brain how I feel about it. Regardless of that kiss with Elliot, I keep getting drawn back to Deacon, but he needs to know what really happened the day we broke up, the day everything fell apart.

"Dea, about your proposal."

He groans as he runs a hand through his hair. "It's okay. We don't have to do this."

I rest my hand over his, stopping his nervous movement and causing him to focus on me. "Yes, we do. I freaked, and not because I didn't love you, and it certainly wasn't because I was in love with someone else." I glance down at my left hand, thinking I could have an engagement ring on my finger, and this could be our honeymoon had I not overreacted. "I have one failed marriage under my belt already. The next time I walk down that aisle, I want to be completely sure about it."

He rubs a thumb over the back of my hand, releasing the tension in the conversation.

"What would it take for you to be completely ready?"

I let his question sink in while I close my eyes. All I hear are seagulls flitting around the shoreline and people chatting at tables close by. "I don't know."

Deacon's shoulders slump, but he recovers quickly as he nods. "I'm sorry if I jumped the gun, and we could have talked about it, but then *he* showed up at the restaurant... and I let my insecurities get the best of me, and... here we are."

"About the ring... It was exquisite and perfect. I hope you got a refund."

He shakes his head, and I am officially the worst ex-girlfriend on the planet.

"It was custom made... Let's talk about something else." He clears his throat.

"Since we are 'clearing the air,' can I tell you something else?"

"Of course. Confession is good for the soul." His strained expression makes me feel like he's not sure he really wants to know.

My next words need to be chosen carefully because we seem to have turned a corner in our relationship—or friendship, at least. "Those were text messages from Elliot that night."

He stiffens and looks away as his jaw muscles work overtime. "I don't think I want to hear any more."

I tap his hand. "But you always knew I was still friends with him. I never kept that from you."

He slides his hand away from mine and sips from his glass of water.

"Elliot was selling me his season tickets to the Crooners. It was for your birthday. I wanted to do something without my father's help or money."

My heart throbs in my ears while I wait for him to react. He nods as he absorbs my words. His expression is unreadable.

I can't stand the silence, so I yammer on. "And just so you know, I've been giving the tickets away these past few weeks because every time I go there... Well, you know. It's too hard. I keep seeing us on that ice in our stupid duck costumes."

I assume that memory flashes through his brain too, because he shakes his head then playfully throws his napkin at me. "We're a couple of idiots."

"From a guy's perspective, do you think I've been giving Elliot mixed messages about our 'friendship'?" I hate using air quotes, but I think it's appropriate in this situation.

"Yep."

The way he didn't have to even think about it makes me feel like I'm terrible at reading the signs flashing right in front of my face. "I didn't mean to, but after he kissed me, that's what's been buzzing around in my brain. Maybe he can't friendzone me after we've had such an... intimate past."

"It's not your problem. It's so easy to fall in love with you. I don't fault the guy. I just wish... I wish he wasn't here."

"Me too."

"And..." He stares off, almost like he's afraid to scare me off again. "I miss you so much. I know I messed things up, but if given another chance, I will never doubt you again."

Tears prickle my eyes, and I bat them away before he can see my reaction. His words soak into my soul, and I am so overcome with emotions that if we don't stop this truth telling, I may melt into a puddle of tears. "I like that we're clearing the air. Not keeping any secrets."

His face pales, and I'm afraid he's going to throw up. "There are things you don't know about me... things that happened a long time ago that I'm not proud of."

"Dea, we have all done things that we're not too thrilled about. I married a man I wasn't in love with just to please my parents. Can you top that?"

He spits out a chuckle as he bites his bottom lip.

"I'm sure whatever is on your mind is insignificant now. It's in the past. Don't ruin our happy bubble."

Storm clouds form in his expression before he clears his throat. He stares off, his lips forming a thin line as he nods slightly.

To lighten the mood, I say, "Since we have cleared the air, can I see my ring?" When he snaps his head in my direction, I wink.

"Your ring?"

"The ring that I almost had."

"No, you cannot see it. Let's get out of here."

While he pays, I send a message to April.

Me: Spending the entire day with Deacon. *heart emoji*

April: *heart-eyes smiley face emoji*

April: Can you two kiss and make up already???

Me: Speaking of kissing, Elliot kissed me yesterday.

April: Gross. Can't you pay one of the LARPers to "accidentally" push him off the ship?

Me: *eyeroll emoji* Hugs.

Deacon holds out a hand to help me rise from my chair.

Then I snatch up my bags and adjust my new hat. "I have an idea."

"What's that?" His thumb rubs the back of my hand, which makes me momentarily lose my train of thought.

"We could buy me a friendship ring. What do you think? We are friends, right? I really miss you, Dea."

He smiles and brushes my braid over my shoulder then takes a step closer. His expression is dark and smoldering. "I guess I have room for one more... friend in my life, so let's get you a friendship ring. My treat."

My eyebrows rise while I shoot him a feigned shocked expression. "Deacon Youngblood, this sea air is good for you."

"Don't ruin it."

He tries to act all broody, but I see that slight grin forming on the side of his mouth as I squeeze his hand, and I rest my head on his shoulder. This is the best day of the cruise. Tonight, we set sail again for Miami, then we'll be back to our normal lives, whatever that may entail. I don't want anything to ruin the last few days at sea because today has been magical, even if it started out a little rough.

Chapter Seventeen

Deacon

After an hour of window shopping, she pulls me into a store that's no more than a shack. If I sneeze hard, the whole thing will tumble down on us. She picks out matching T-shirts that say Cruisin' for a Bruisin.

"Nope, I prefer this one." I show her the Let's Get Ship-Faced ones, and she high-fives me.

"We must wear them to dinner tonight so we can be all matchy-matchy."

My eyebrows rise. "Oh, so we're going to dinner tonight, huh?"

"I have no specific plans. You?" She tries to hide her bashful grin behind a strand of hair that has fallen loose from her braid.

Just to make her squirm a little, I mull it over as if I have lots of things scheduled for tonight. "I'll pencil you in."

Chrissy lets out a husky chuckle. "Thanks for the generosity." And mocking me, she adds, "I'll pencil you in too."

I tap the glass over the jewelry display. "These would make sweet friendship rings."

She rushes over to the case, hip-bumping me out of the way. The choices are nothing more than tourist trinkets, but that's Chris. She's not flashy like Angela. In fact, the engagement ring I bought is something she would never have picked out for herself. For someone who has been surrounded by money all her life, she isn't consumed by it.

She giggles as she tries on several different silver rings with either turquoise or wampum. I point at a cute one in the shape of a mermaid tail.

"Eh, it's pretty but not exactly what I'm looking for. Oooh. This is it." She points at a simple white-and-pink ring made from a shell, something she could get at any dime store in town, but by the way she bounces up and down, this is indeed the one. "Isn't it perfect?"

"If it's what you want, then it is."

After I purchase the little ring along with the Ship-Faced T-shirts, we walk down the street, taking in all the sights and smells of the dock. Seagulls swoop down to the water in search of snacks while the waves slosh toward shore. I never knew there were so many shades of blue, but the ocean's colors vary as far as the eye can see.

I stop to pull the ring out of the little bag. She turns around and when I drop to one knee, the color from her face drains. Flashbacks of our proposal dinner fiasco rush through my brain, and by the way the blood drained from her face, I think she's having the same moment.

"What are you doing?" She glances around at the crowd that's formed around us, phones out to film the event.

"Priscilla Christine Parks, will you be my... friend?" I never imagined using the *friend* word, but here I am, taking baby steps because I certainly don't want to scare her away again.

The crowd groans and slinks away like I messed up their entire day.

But Chrissy throws her head back and lets out the loudest giggle. "Of course, Deacon Michael Youngblood. I will forever be your friend and your partner in any contest as long as it includes a duck suit."

She holds out her left hand, but I pull her right hand down and place the shell ring on her ring finger, making her roll her eyes. The way she gazes at it, I wonder if she wishes it was *the* ring, *the* ring that is in our stateroom right now.

Before I can allow myself to pull her in for a kiss, I clear my throat. "Come on. We're burning daylight." I pick up her packages and meander toward more street vendors with her by my side.

I glance at my phone to show the time. "It's almost three o'clock. We should start back toward the ship, or we might get left behind."

Chrissy stares down as she adjusts her big, floppy hat. "Yeah. That would be horrible, right?"

I'm actually thinking we could have a fabulous time hanging out on this island, just the two of us. We could buy a shack, sell trinkets, and watch the sun set over the ocean every night. I could get used to that life.

My phone buzzes, ending my fairy-tale dreams. I pull up the message, and it's from Angela. I ignore it because I don't want to deal with her right now. That's not the best move for her sponsor, but she'll be fine.

We walk back to the dock in silence, me carrying an armload of shopping bags. Chrissy can't keep her eyes off the silly ring I gave her. God, I wish I had the courage to really propose, but if I've learned anything, it's that timing is everything.

Securely on deck of the LARP Boat again, she blows a kiss toward Kings Wharf. "Goodbye, Bermuda. I'll never forget you."

We enter the cabin, full of packages. I collapse on the bed, and Chrissy lands on the sofa, flopping off her shoes.

"I forgot how you can wear me out with shopping," I say.

She laughs. "Well, you can wear me out too."

Fun! I cock an eyebrow, hoping she will continue with this interesting confession.

Chrissy chuckles. "I don't mean physically. I mean mentally, but physically, too, if we are being completely honest."

That's an interesting way to end a perfectly fun day together. "That's my job."

She rummages around in her packages and holds up a sun dress then checks her reflection in the mirror. "Well, you're good at what you do. Wow." She stares at the ceiling. "I have no filter today."

I'm not complaining.

Her mouth turns down as she stares at her purchases. "I can't believe we set sail tonight, heading back to Miami. It's all coming to an end so fast."

"We have one more full day at sea. Make the most of it before we're landlocked again."

Chrissy nods, and I wish I could read her mind. After she blows out her breath, she stares at me for a moment. "I think I'm going to take a walk around the ship. I have a lot on my mind."

Was I too forward today? Did she think I was pressuring her to get back together? If she only knew how much I was holding back, she would appreciate how *not* forward I'm being. Not waiting for me to ask if I can join her for fear of making things worse, she leaves our stateroom. I could go after her, but I don't want to disturb her if she's sorting out her feelings. That sounds presumptuous of me, to think the only thing weighing heavily on her mind would be me, but maybe today reminded her how good we are together. I hope so.

Lying on my back, I stare at the ceiling. Three blasts from the cruise ship signal that we're about to depart from Bermuda. It was a perfect day. I only wish I knew what I did to make Chrissy skitter off like that.

My phone buzzes again, breaking me out of my thoughts. It's another message from Angela.

Angela: SOS

With a groan, I think of all the scenarios that could cause such a short but frantic message. Is she being tempted to drink? Did she go ashore, and the ship is going to leave her? If that's the case, texting me a cryptic cry for help isn't going to make any difference. The ship's policy is to wait for no one.

Angela: Hello??? Need help!

I rise from the bed to leave even though I am not in the mood to help anyone right now.

Me: Where are you?

Lost in my thoughts about where Chrissy could have gone, I don't watch where I'm going when I enter the elevator. One of the guys stumbles backward and bumps up against the back wall. "Dude. You almost hit my wench."

"My bad, Frodo."

"Actually, if you want to compare me to a Lord of the Rings character, I would appreciate it if you would consider calling me Gandalf."

His companions nod in agreement.

Getting flustered, I yell, "Understood!"

The girl slides her hand into a leather pouch and pulls out a handful of birdseed and flings it on me.

I sputter as I spit some out. "What the heck?"

"Magic dust. You need it."

The elevator door opens, and I exit in front of them. "You're going to need something more than that."

"I have an idea," one LARPer says to me. "You should join us today. It's a great way to work off your frustrations."

"As much fun as that seems, I think I'll pass."

They back off, and I storm past them in search of Angela while another text comes in from her.

Angela: I'm not drinking, but I can't stop playing the slots. This is so much fun!!

The casino! I race through the ship, up to the Celebration deck, and past the theater where a medieval sketch is taking place. I burst into the casino, overwhelmed by all the chatter and bells chiming from the machines. From the entrance, I hear Angela's distinctive *woo-hoo*ing and run toward her voice. She's sitting at a slot machine, a sparkly silver cowboy hat on her head, surrounded by LARPers cheering her on. Lights flash as money flows from the machine in front of her.

When she sees me, she throws her hands out wide. "This is way more fun than getting drunk. Want to join me?"

"No." I take her by the hand to lead her away. She snatches it out of my grasp to snag her plastic bucket of winnings.

"Deacon, meet my new friends. Duma Proud, Nardpro— "

"It's Narpor. I'm a dark knight." He holds out a hand for me to shake.

Angela giggles. "Sorry. I keep getting that wrong." She points at the third guy, dressed as an elf. "And this cutie pie is Seredi."

"Don't forget me." Charmaine hugs Angela.

"Silly me. You're the best."

"You are."

They giggle like old friends, then Charmaine smiles at me. "I think we met earlier. Pink nails, right?"

Cringing, I hope she doesn't go into any details. Charmaine points from me to Angela. "You two know each other?"

"Long story."

Charmaine's jaw drops, but she quickly snaps it closed as she plops down at a slot machine.

I motion with my head. "Come on, Ange. Let's go." I've got to get her back to her cabin without running into Chrissy. I doubt this would be where she clears her head, but that would be just my luck. After the wonderful day we had ashore, I don't want to mess things up now.

Angela hugs her winnings to her chest as I escort her from the casino. "Trading one addiction for another is not healthy. You know that."

She snatches her arm away from me and halts in the middle of the casino. "I messaged you because I was going stir crazy. You didn't respond, so I went to the one place I figure I wouldn't run into Chrissy." She holds out her bucket of winnings. "Want some?"

Charmaine acts like she's playing the slots, but she leans closer to us like she's trying to overhear.

"No, I don't." I run a hand through my hair. "I was spending the day with Chrissy, if you must know."

Angela squeals. "That's awesome. Did you have fun? Are you making progress? Tell me. I want all the details."

"I've made some progress."

"That's great. Can I help speed things along?"

A chuckle escapes my lips. "Stay in your room. That's what you can do."

Angela pouts as she stares down at her winnings. "Buzzkill."

"Please go back to your room." I peer around, hoping Chrissy hasn't followed me down here.

Angela stomps the floor like a petulant child. "Fine." She marches away, and I hope she's headed to her stateroom and not the bar.

On the way back to my cabin, I stop by the pool deck. After buying a fitness magazine, I slump down into a lounge chair to WhatsApp my brother. When his face appears, his smile fades as his brow scrunches up.

"Bro, what crawled up your butt and died?"

As hard as it is to admit everything, I tell him everything about my day: how it was amazing, but then Chrissy left to think, and that Angela is on board, and it's all going to blow up in my face if I don't watch it.

"Okay, little brother. That's all well and good, but what did you buy me?"

"You suck."

Drake chuckles but adds, "Sorry. I was only trying to lighten up the mood."

"I'm in love with Chrissy, but I'm afraid if she finds out Angela is here, she'll never believe the reason."

"You'll get no argument from me, dude. It just looks bad. Take a walk on deck to think about what you want and how you want to get it. You need to chill for a while and formulate a plan for how you're going to unpickle yourself."

Never in a million years did I think my perpetual bachelor brother could be so wise.

Chapter Eighteen

Chrissy

While I watch the LARPers do their thing, flitting about the bow of the ship, I wonder what it's like to just enjoy life without a care in the world. These people run around with foam swords and plastic shields, wearing makeshift costumes, and don't care one iota if anyone laughs at them. They are totally unfazed by the world around them. Before this trip, so much time had passed since I last had fun that I think I forgot how. Swimming with the dolphins was amazing, but it wasn't because I was with Elliot. But today... everything Deacon and I did together was even more special because he was there beside me.

Then we came back to the cabin, and I felt like I was being stifled again, like I'm being forced to make some major life-changing decisions. I'm sure Deacon thinks I freaked out again, just like the night he proposed. He's not putting any pressure on me—it's all coming from inside my brain. But at least this time, Deacon didn't run after me. He's giving me space to think.

I slip closer to the LARP event as two fairies flit around me. One has gold wings and a burgundy dress with a gold corset. The other one wears a crown of flowers in her hair, and her gauzy dress flows freely in the ocean breeze.

"Want to join us today?" the one in the burgundy costume asks. I glance around behind myself just in case they weren't talking to me.

I point at myself. "Me?"

"Sure."

A flush creeps up my neck as I imagine myself doing something so completely out of my element and looking like a fool. "No, thank you. Maybe next time."

But they do seem to be having way more fun than me, so maybe their hobby isn't so hokey after all.

She waves her wand over my head as the other one dances around me. "If you change your mind, just follow the Celtic sounds to be transported to another dimension."

"It's tempting."

"What's the harm? You're on a ship with a bunch of strangers. Let loose and have a good time. You can go back to your normal self when we get back to the land of boring the day after tomorrow."

"I'll think about it."

They prance off hand in hand, and I almost change my mind to follow them. With closed eyes, I hold on to the railing and take a deep breath, letting the gentle motion of the ship center me. The salty air whips my hair around my face. When I feel something touch my hand, I fling open my eyes to see Elliot standing next to me.

Do I have a tracker device implanted so he can find me at the most inopportune times?

"Hey. I tried to find you today to go ashore with me, but you didn't answer your phone."

He's right. I noticed he sent me several messages, but I didn't feel the need to respond. Even though I don't owe him an explanation, I reply, "I went ashore with Deacon today."

Out of the corner of my eye, I notice his knuckles turn white as he grips the railing.

Elliot chuckles then shakes his head. "So, have you two gotten back together?"

Have we? I don't know. I think we were headed in that direction when I had to "get some air." I'm not telling Elliot that because he'll assume I have doubts about Deacon. It's never been about Deacon. I was always the problem.

I respond with a slight shrug. "It's not that simple."

Elliot takes that as an invitation and asks, "Would you like to have dinner with me tonight?"

Words don't form in my mouth as he waits for my reply. His request doesn't sound like two friends enjoying a meal together. What he's not saying is louder, and I'm afraid to know his real intentions. But maybe what Deacon says about Elliot is true, and there's only one way to find out.

"What is up with you?" I ask.

"Isn't it obvious? I want you back."

His words shock me into a moment of silence. I guess with his being here, along with that kiss, I assumed that's what he wanted, but for him to say it out loud and so bluntly has me sputtering for a reply.

"No." I have absolutely no feelings for him other than friendship, and the only reason I married him was because my parents wouldn't let me back out of the wedding at the last minute. *What would the neighbors think?* That was the last time I trusted their advice.

"Why not? We could be good together again." He takes me by the hand and leads me to some deck chairs. He plops down in one and flags down the barmaid. "I'll have a beer, please. And my lovely wife here will have... What would you like, honey?"

I take a step back as my brain processes what he just said. With a huff, I reply, "I am his *ex*-wife."

When the barmaid leaves, Elliot says, "Look, I know we parted ways amicably, but—"

Through gritted teeth, I blurt out, "There is no 'but.' We are better off not married, and you know it. There never was a spark or..." I don't want to talk to him about the flippy-floppy feeling because he'll just think I am being silly.

"I never said I was perfect."

"No one is perfect, but our relationship was more of a business transaction, not love."

He shakes his head. "Maybe for you. I understand it may appear as though I was only interested in your family's connections, but I realized I really was in love with you. Still am."

"I never doubted you cared about me, but let's be honest. You are in love with my father." I stare out over the sea, hoping some divine intervention will come to me. I don't want to hurt his feelings, but he still doesn't completely get it. We were never meant to be anything more than friends.

"Ouch, and not true. Not completely."

"Even if I was the least bit interested in getting back with you... which I'm not... the success rate of a return to a failed marriage is reduced by fifty percent."

He chuckles. "You have statistics for every situation. You should write a fortune cookie with that stat."

Shrugging, I slide a wispy strand of hair behind my ear as I ignore his dig about what I do for a living. "You can't deny the figures."

He cocks his head to the side then takes my hand in his. "What's this?"

"It's a friendship ring. Deacon bought it for me today."

"Looks cheap." That sourpuss face tells me he thinks it's more than just a cheap piece of costume jewelry.

I snatch my hand out of his and stare down at the shell ring. "Thanks for the insult. I picked it out."

Elliot scans the deck area, and I follow his gaze to see Deacon standing on the upper deck. As soon as Deacon catches us watching him, he turns his attention to his phone. Elliot takes my hand again. The contact revolts me, so I try to extricate it from his tight grip.

"Please have dinner with me tonight."

Not taking my gaze from Deacon, I shake my head.

"It must get lonely eating alone."

With that comment, I snatch my hand out of his.

He holds his hands up in surrender. "Okay. No dinner. How about rock climbing? You like that. Nothing sexual. Just friends." His sarcastic tone is not lost on me.

"I'll pass." To get him to back off, I spit out the dumbest thing ever before I can stop myself. "I'm going LARPing."

He sputters and falls into a fit of laughter. "You? Good one."

His chuckles slice through me, and I can't form a reply. When he realizes I don't find his reply funny, he clears his throat and swallows the last of his chuckles.

"I still have my costume, and you can't deny how good I look in it." He waggles his eyes while I roll mine.

"That was not an invitation to join me." I'm not really going, but if he thinks I am, he'll be out of my way for a while, maybe until we disembark in Miami.

"I'm just kidding. Dressing up and doing one silly dance was one thing. I'm not going to waste my night in Middle Earth. I hear the casino calling my name."

I watch Elliot leave, and when he makes eye contact with Deacon, he does a girly wave. Deacon just shakes his head. This nonlove triangle is exhausting. I feel like making them both walk the plank.

Chapter Nineteen

By the time I get back to my stateroom, I've settled my nerves. This is going to work out. I just need to not rush it with Chrissy. But when I notice the door is ajar, I screech to a halt. *Is he in there?*

Tentatively, I slide it open to find Chrissy pacing as she mumbles to herself. All I catch is "Elliot" and "fortune cookies," but the rest is too low to make out. I enter without saying a word and slump down on the sofa while she has her one-sided conversation.

Trying to break the tension, which could be cut with a knife, I say, "I don't know about you, but I was having more fun ashore."

She sits beside me as she runs her fingers through her hair, removing the braid. "Am I giving him mixed messages?"

That's obvious, but it's cute that she doesn't think so.

I let out a chuckle. "Pretty much." The last thing I want to do right now is give her dating advice.

She pokes me in the ribs. "Why can't a girl and a guy be friends without any hidden meaning, without the guy thinking every single nice comment gives them the green light to hook up?"

Not going there. I cock an eyebrow and focus on my phone because I do not even know how to respond to that.

"Never mind. You don't have to answer that. But you're still friends with Angela, right?"

The collar of my T-shirt suddenly tightens around my neck. This could be an innocent question, or she could have a hidden meaning while trying to get me to fess up. When I open my mouth to disclose the little Angela factoid, she stops me with a hand.

She waves me off. "But I don't see her waltzing around the ship, confessing her undying love to you." Chrissy does a full-body shiver.

My phone tumbles out of my hand and lands on my foot, and I let out a yelp.

She picks it up and hands it to me. "Are you alright?"

Don't look at the screen. Don't look at the screen.

She turns toward me, and her knee brushes against mine. "I want to make sure you understand something." She holds up one finger. "I did not invite him here." With two fingers up, she adds, "I didn't encourage the kiss, and thirdly, he is my friend. I have never seen him act so possessive. I don't know what's come over him."

I do. *He wants you back as much as I do.* And I've seen it in his eyes every time he's around her. She's just never paid attention before now.

"Neither do I." I hope she picks up on my sarcasm because I laid it on thick.

Chrissy plays with the friendship ring, turning it in circles on her finger. "He asked me to dinner, but I turned him down."

Yes!

"I told him I was going LARPing."

"Excuse me?"

She giggles. "Yep. It was to throw him for a loop, but I actually might go. Sounds kind of fun, doing something completely different."

"I would love to see you dressed up as a sexy medieval maiden. I'm sure there's something in your closet that would work."

She nudges me with her elbow, then her mouth turns up in a sly grin. "You should come too."

"No way. I'd look completely out of place."

"Come on," she says, shoving me on the shoulder. "It'll be fun."

She stands to check her reflection in the mirror then grabs some clothes out of the drawer. With the wench costume held against herself, she swishes the skirt around. While she dresses in front of me, I sit and mull over what she's about to do.

"Last chance." Her singsong voice grates on my nerves. With a shrug of her shoulders, she adds, "I'm going to have some fun."

I wonder why I can't just step out of my comfort zone and live a little. It won't matter if I'm a dork if I'm with Chrissy. It could lead to stories we tell our grandchildren about.

"If you change your mind, just follow the flute music to the event." And with that, she leaves.

I groan as I punch the pillow. Sitting there in silence isn't helping anything, so I grab my phone and message my brother.

Me: Are you up?

Drake: I am now.

Me: Nothing is going like I thought. Nothing. At. All.

My phone beeps, and I see my brother's face, then my sister appears too. For the next ten minutes, I rehash my ordeal and how I'm trying to hide Angela though everything is working against me. Bailey doubles over with giggles while Drake does his best to hide his smile, but I know he's one second from busting out into a fit of laughter.

"I thought you two were making progress."

"So did I, but Chrissy just left to go LARPing."

Drake's mouth drops open, then an evil grin slides across his face. "What are you waiting for? Go hang out with the LARPers."

Bailey shoves Drake out of the frame. "Go. Get dressed up in a costume and win her back. It'll be fun. Show her your playful side."

When I say it, it sounds stupid, but how Bailey puts it makes total sense. It's not about making a fool of myself or knowing what I'm doing. It's about having a good time, just like the bathtub race while wearing a duck costume was. If I could do that, this is simple. I feel stupid for not jumping at the chance to do something silly again with Chrissy.

Drake says off camera, "I was only kidding."

"I'm not." I log off before he can talk me out of it. The LARPers seem harmless, and I may just find a new pastime. I wonder if they sell foam swords aboard this ship. I leap off the sofa in search of the role-playing event. As soon as I exit the elevator, I bump right into Charmaine decked out in a black sundress with a shawl attached to her wrists. When she sees me, she stretches out her arms to reveal blue-and-black butterfly wings.

"Isn't this the cutest?"

"It's great. I am so glad I ran into you because I need your help."

She holds my hands to inspect my nails. "What prank did she pull this time?"

"Nothing. She's LARPing today. I need to be there to show her I can have fun."

Charmaine eyes me from head to toe. "Are you going to wear *that?*"

Staring down at my normal, nonLARPish clothing, I reply, "That's what I need help with."

She takes me by the arm and leads me down the concourse. "Come with me. I think your LARP name should be something strong and powerful like Dunntosity or..." Her eyes get big. "I've got it. Grishork, the Sea Demon."

I mull over her words then shrug. "I could go with that."

She yammers on about LARP rules and how the players must speak what's happening all while they are doing it, and it sounds like she's been part of this group her entire life instead of just a few days. We stop in front of a shop that's been transformed into a fantasy world. It spills over with people picking out items for their last-minute costumes. At least I'm in good company.

Charmaine flips through a rack of vintage clothing items. "Let's see, I think you need something dark and mysterious to contrast that dirty blond hair." She holds up a black jacket that looks like a cross between something Prince would wear in concert and a pirate outfit. The silver embroidery gives it a goth vibe.

"It'll accentuate your broad shoulders and small waist. You'll need a sword too." She shoves the jacket into my hands and rushes over to the weaponry section—how odd that sounds on a cruise ship. She tosses me a foam sword and says, "You'll need a do-rag to complete the outfit. All that's left now is a backstory. We can work on that as we go."

Staring at the stuff she's shoved in my arms, I shake my head. "Don't you think this is a bit overkill? It's just one night."

She winks. "That's what we all say. Get changed. I promise you will be a new man in more ways than one."

Charmaine is not going to take no for an answer, so I grab an empty changing room and slip on the jacket. When I catch my reflection in the mirror, I'm not dissatisfied with what I see. She's right. I really do feel as if I've stepped back in time to a land before the modern world, where sea demons terrorized ships and rescued helpless damsels. I adjust the head covering as Charmaine hands me the sword.

"Dayum. If she doesn't want you, I do."

Awkward. She's old enough to be my aunt, so that's not going to happen, not on this planet and not even in a fantasy world.

She giggles. "Now, when you strike someone, you yell, 'Lightning bolt, lightning bolt!'"

I playfully pop her on the shoulder with the foam sword. "Lightning bolt."

"Louder."

At the top of my lungs, I repeat the mantra until she's satisfied with my enthusiasm.

Charmaine nods her approval then says, "Let's go get your girl." She leads the way as she yells, "Courage, wisdom, power!"

Chapter Twenty

Chrissy

I'm going to wear a hole in the decking as I pace. Getting dressed up for this LARP event was the easy part. Passing to that side of the ship to role-play is a totally different level. This may have been a bad idea, but I'm here now.

"Hey there." Elliot saunters up to me like he doesn't have a care in the world. My shoulders slump as I regret telling him I may be here. Now, I really do need to leave.

He eyes me up and down, making me feel underdressed. I glance down to make sure my breasts are still tucked nicely inside my wench costume. No need to give him the wrong idea. He's decked out in his LARP costume and carries his mask as he bows low. Cute, but he's still Elliot, no matter how much he pretends to be someone else.

I throw my hands in the air. "Why are you here?"

"You invited me."

"I did no such thing."

"You look amazing. Let's go have some fun."

Maybe the LARP venue will be so big that we can "accidentally" get separated. We turn a corner, and it's like we stepped back in time. Fake plants cover the deck rails, illuminated wreaths hang from the walls, and flute music lilts through this part of the ship.

A guy with plastic elf ears passes by, wearing a steampunk top hat and brown vest. He carries a plastic stick with a spear tip on the end made of silver duct tape. "Welcome to the Collision of the Sea. I'm Edmond Orlich, the dark elf explorer." Edmond looks us over then adds "And you are...?"

Elliot fidgets, which is the best part of this ordeal. "I am Targ, and this is—"

"Calico, the Fortune Maker. We want to join in on your little game."

Edmond swings his plastic sword like he's Conan the Barbarian. "A game is something you aim to win. LARPing is more than a game. It's a lifestyle."

My ex always appears put together and in command of his surroundings, but right now, he's so out of his element. I gulp. "My bad. How can we...? We want to learn."

"Calypso!" Edmond yells at a small, frumpy woman. She wears a white cover-up. Her face is painted in black markings around her old lady glasses, and her straw hat almost swallows her head. She sings to us, "Let us drink and be merry." Her voice is high and somewhat off pitch. "Welcome."

"We don't know how to do all of this." Elliot glances at me, and I nod.

"Come with me. You, sweetie, can be NPC today." She takes me by an arm. I glance over my shoulder to find Elliot standing there like a bump on a log. *Yay!* My wish came true. I may not see him anymore tonight.

To Calypso, I say, "I want a sword."

"NPCs don't battle."

Then what's the point? I have no idea what she's talking about. "I apologize for not being prepared." I point at Elliot, who is chatting with a fairy. "His name is Elliot, and you definitely do not want to know his... backstory."

An elf prances by in a deep-purple costume with her hair pulled back into a long sloppy braid. She retrieves bird seed from a leather pouch on her belt and sprinkles it everywhere. "Shield of courage."

An older woman dressed in all black with blue-and-black butterfly wings flits by, and my mouth drops.

"Charmaine? Is that you?"

She winks then swishes a finger under my nose. "Charmaine is not here. In this area of the ship, I am Thalassa, a bright witch."

"I thought you chose Freesia."

She waves me off. "It didn't suit my character. This stuff is so much fun. In fact, I may join the Charlotte Regional LARPers Association when I get home. I've been working on my backstory. How does this sound?"

She clears her throat and throws back her shoulders. "I was once a servant wench until Thayer saved my life, so now, I repay him by spreading magic everywhere I go." She flings bird seed in front of me. "I know it's super basic right now, but that's all the time I had to make something up. It's a work in progress. I'll add as I go. Don't you just adore this corset?" She throws her boobs in my face, making me take a step back. "It pushes the girls up. I may never take it off."

"Seems like you've found your calling."

Charmaine waves. "Gotta go. Have fun today. Oh, one more thing." She leans in close, like the information is for my ears only. "I hear there is a sea demon you may want to... confront."

Before she leaves, I grab her hands. "What does that mean? Should I be scared?"

"Definitely not scared. You'll see soon enough."

"I'm an NPC. That's good for me, right?"

"It's a good way to start. You keep up with damages—eight and the person's dead. But even if you die, you can come back to life if someone with magic like me saves you. If that happens and you come back to life, you must start over as a new character." She shivers. "I don't have enough brain capacity to have another backstory ready, so I'm hoping I don't die. NPCs hand out to-do lists and give info to the PCs."

"Wow. You've learned a lot in a couple of days."

"I know. It's so much fun. Toodles."

"Wait!" I yell at her retreating frame.

She vanishes among the costumed characters, yelling, "Courage, wisdom, power!" as she passes by people slapping foam and plastic swords around like they're duking it out to the death.

After one guy gets whacked on the arm with a sword, he tucks it behind himself. "Strike to the forearm. Aw, curses."

Calypso hands me a clipboard, and I follow her, noting hits and when characters die. They seem to take it well afterward as they cheer from the sidelines. I thought the combat would be a free-for-all, but the LARPers play by the rules, and Calypso is very patient with my lack of knowledge. She explains when a character is permanently dead. I guess magic doesn't work on them anymore. For the next hour, I do my best to stay close to her and mimic her movements. I even let out a *woo-hoo* or two when someone escapes certain death.

To capture the moment, I slide my phone out of my pocket to take a photo. Calypso gives me a huge stink eye. "Even noncharacters shouldn't use tech props. It's rude."

"Sorry. I was just checking the time."

"Time is never-ending here."

"Of course. What was I thinking?"

Two fighters start going at it around me, and I dart from one side to the other to get out of their way. The man in the black jacket swings around, and I notice it's Deacon.

Wait. What?

"Spitting venom!" he yells with the sternest expression.

"Augh," the other guy says as he takes a jab at Deacon.

"Ow. Poison damage."

"Burning blade."

One guy falls to the floor. "I'm knocked out." He rolls on the ground toward me. "Protected by the shield of courage."

Deacon catches my eye and winks. "Hey, there." His voice is so bashful and not in keeping with his LARP character. He bows low then says, "I'm Grishork, a sea demon. I'm here to protect this ship from the evil forces of Elliotistan. I'm here to rescue a princess named Calico."

I double over laughing at how adorably sexy he looks. That jacket fits snugly against his body, and his head covering gives him a Dread Pirate Roberts vibe. "I didn't know I needed saving from Elliotistan. Did you just make that up? Because that was pretty clever."

He shrugs. "It's not a myth, and you are in grave danger, and only I have the power to save you." Deacon's eyes twinkle as he saunters closer, flicking his wrist to rotate his sword.

Scuffling behind me gets closer until Elliot pushes me out of the way to shoot Deacon in the chest with a foam arrow. It bounces off Deacon and pops a random guy in the back of the head.

"Poison damage," Elliot says.

Deacon slumps his shoulders. "Dude. Seriously? We were having a moment here."

As Elliot circle-strafes Deacon, he snaps another arrow, popping Deacon in the back.

"Ow. Not necessary. I'm obviously dead already."

I check my clipboard and say to Elliot, "I think that's against the rules."

"I. Don't. Care." He flings another arrow toward Deacon.

Dea ducks in time for it to miss him. Then in slow motion, with all his might, he rushes Elliot, knocking him off his feet. "Lightning bolt!"

The two scuffle, and with one last shove, Elliot stumbles backward and into me. I slip on the birdseed magic dust and backpedal, tripping over a shield. The birdseed under my shoe makes my body go one way and my foot another, twisting my ankle. When I fall on my butt, I let out a string of curse words. My foot turns at an angle not normal for any human.

"Stop. Getting. In. My. Way." Deacon punctuates every word by ripping arrows out of Elliot's quiver.

Elliot manages to crouch in a kneeling position, doing his best to deflect the sea demon's sword. "I'm here for *her*." He points at me still sprawled out on the deck.

"So am I." Deacon stands, his fake sword hovering over Elliot's chest. "The difference is I'm in love with Chrissy, and you're in love with the *idea* of Chrissy."

All the noise and chaos of the fight scene vanishes as I stare at both of them. None of us move or make a sound. My throat closes as Deacon's confession washes over me. His words ring true. He's in love with *me*, while Elliot loves the idea of me. It's like all the pieces of the puzzle fit now. I've known this all along, but the way Deacon worded it makes so much sense.

Deacon scans the deck, and when he sees me lying on the floor, his eyes grow dark. He rushes over to me with Elliot not far behind.

Calypso rushes to me. "You aren't supposed to be in character."

"I'm not."

With ease, Deacon scoops me up in his arms then says, "Aw, curses."

Through gritted teeth, I say, "I'm okay."

"If you reinjured that ankle, I'll never forgive myself."

"It's not that bad."

It hurts like the devil, but I'll be okay if I can just walk it off. But being in Deacon's arms again causes my brain to go fuzzy. If he's willing, he can carry me everywhere.

Chapter Twenty-One

Deacon

Elliot stands there helpless as I walk toward the exit, carrying Chrissy. A cursory view of her ankle lets me know I don't think she sprained or tore anything, but with her history, I don't want to take any chances. She needs to elevate her foot and apply ice to ensure it doesn't get any worse.

"I think I'm okay." Chrissy wriggles in my arms but doesn't insist I put her down.

"Let me help her." Elliot shoves his way into our space and attempts to take her out of my arms.

"I've got this. If you don't remember, my specialty is sports injuries. Now, if she needed help with acquiring a company or some financial assistance, I would yield to your expertise."

"Guys, can you two just knock it off?"

Elliot retracts his hands at her harsh words. "I was just trying to help."

After mumbling something, she lets out a breath. "I understand, but Deacon does know what he's doing."

Happy dance. I don't feel anything broken, so I think it's just a minor, grade-one sprain, not that I'll tell *him* that.

"I landed funny. When you two barbarians were trying to kill each other, I guess I was collateral damage." Chrissy glowers at us while a tear slides down her grimy face. "I fell hard."

Elliot points his bow at me. "Actually, I am still alive, so there." Chrissy and I stare at him until he slumps his shoulders. "I was having a blast until this guy messed things up."

Chrissy waves him off. "I tripped over you, but by all means, don't let me stop you from having fun. Go."

After I swipe a strand of hair away from her face, I rest my forehead against hers. "Are you ready to call it a day?"

She wraps her arms around my neck and squeezes me like her life depends on it. "Yes, please. That sounds good to me."

Elliot scoffs. "Chris, you're such a baby. Suck it up. I thought we were having a good time."

Heat flares in my soul at that idiot's comments. We always take a person's pain level seriously, but he doesn't even think about anything except winning. "Shut up. Do you even know what you are talking about? I'm guessing you don't."

"She's always so dramatic, just a way to get attention. She has serious daddy issues."

I don't know who is more shocked at his words, me or Chrissy, because we both suck in audible gasps. That was low, and if he's trying to win Chrissy back, he's going in the wrong direction. Take it from someone who has made a thousand mistakes with this woman. Insulting her and rubbing her father issues in her face is not going to win him any brownie points.

After a long beat of silence, Chrissy shifts in my arms and tells him, "And people wonder why I divorced you."

He plucks a red rose from a nearby planter and sticks it out for Chrissy to take, like it's a peace offering. "Don't you remember the good ol' days?"

"The good ol' days?" She sputters out a disgusted chuckle as she pushes the rose away. "You never paid the slightest bit of attention to what I prefer. I'll admit there are worse things to be bad at, but every now and then, would it have killed you to pay attention? I'm not saying there weren't good times, but it just wasn't enough. We've been over this already. We're so much better suited to be friends. I don't love you."

He takes a step closer to her, making me stand taller, ready to protect Chrissy at all costs. "Of course you love me." He shrugs and adds, "And your father adores me. By the way. He would be so disappointed in you right now."

The LARPers gradually stop fighting as they see this more interesting event taking place among them. Some slap their palms with their swords like they are ready to take on Whitaker if given the go-ahead. Not intervening takes all my willpower too, because telling a woman you know what's best for her is not cool. But this is a battle she must win on her own. If she says the word, I'll be on him in a second, and it appears like she has an entire swarm of LARPers ready to back her up too.

Chrissy's face is so red that I'm surprised she hasn't burst into flames. In a slow, methodical motion, she unlaces her hands from behind my neck and wriggles out of my hold. When she stands straight, with fierceness in her eyes, even I take a step back. The warrior has been awakened.

And because Whitaker can't take a hint, he moves closer to her, making some of the LARPers hiss and groan. When he gets within a foot of her, she straight-arms him.

"No, Elliot. It's not happening."

"What?" He sputters like no one has ever told him no before and it's the most ridiculous word ever. "You led me to believe you wanted to get back together."

She cocks her head to one side. "I did no such thing. You weren't even invited on this cruise in the first place. And just so we are clear, I do not care what my father thinks."

The crowd around us roars with applause. They raise their weapons in celebration like they have won a great war. Whitaker turns in circles like he's about to be attacked. When we lock eyes, I weigh my options. I could punch his lights out, but I don't want to go to LARP jail. Or I could scream in victory since the Sea Demon seems to have won this round, but that's not my style. So I stand still in my place and reply with a slow, over-the-top golf clap, and his eyes narrow into slits, telling me I hit my target. And when Chrissy slaps her hands like she's clearing dust away, I can't contain my smile anymore.

Hobbling slightly, she walks back to me and wraps her arms around my neck to pull me into a massive kiss, causing all the LARPers to go wild. I slide my arms around her waist to pull her close, not caring that we have an audience.

Nibbling on my ear, she whispers, "Let's get out of here."

Music to my ears.

I crouch down for her to hop on my back.

"I can walk."

"Of course you can, but where's the fun in that?"

She snorts, so I take it that she's already recovering from the mishap. After I adjust her on my back, I grasp behind her knees and stand.

Getting one last jab in, Whitaker yells, "Chrissy, you'll regret this!"

"I highly doubt it." I love the confidence in her words.

With applause rising behind us, I leave the event with Chrissy riding piggyback. As she wraps her arms around my neck to stabilize herself, she snickers. "Lightning bolt?"

I grin as I tighten my grip on her. "It was something Charmaine said I should use to get into character. I think it worked, because it was fun kicking his butt, but as expected, he plays by his own rules."

"Please, I don't want to talk about Elliot right now."

I don't want her to think, see, or even remember anything about him for a very long time.

As I carry her, I forge a plan to kick Elliot's butt at least five different ways if I ever see him again. The elevator is full of LARPers, but they make room for us by holding their weapons high in the air.

"Curses, what happened?" one asks.

"I just got in the way of the action."

One fairy girl's mouth drops open. "Ooh, I heard in the chat about the NPC getting injured and a fight to avenge a lady." She sprinkles confetti on us.

I spit out several pieces that land in my mouth. "You're famous," I tell Chrissy with a wink.

As the LARPers exit, we fall into a fit of giggles.

"Dea, don't make me laugh. I feel like I had the courage and the wisdom, but I definitely lacked the power."

"I have no idea what you're talking about, but you were so cute. And right now, you need to ice your ankle. Let's get ahead of any swelling."

We explode into the room, and I crouch until her feet hit the floor. She wobbles and hits a picture on the wall. It barely stays in place, and she collapses onto the bed with a groan.

"Man, you were fierce back there. I almost peed my pants. Remind me to never tussle with you when you have that sexy wench outfit on. It does something to you."

She scoffs then shoves my shoulder with her hand. "It did feel good to finally stand up for myself. I should have said those things a long time ago."

My hand covers hers, then our eyes meet. "All that matters is how you are doing. Are you alright?"

She shrugs. "I've been better. I've also been so much worse, so I think I'll live to fight another day. This is nothing compared to the injury you helped me rehab." With a gasp, she adds, "Oh no. Are we back to patient-therapist mode, and you have to wait until I'm cleared before you ask me out?"

My face hurts because of how big my grin is. "If that's the case, I'll sign a document today stating you are completely cleared from any therapy."

I unroll her sock and softly touch her ankle. Chrissy closes her eyes and sighs. She adjusts herself as she reclines on the bed with a groan.

"You need ice to get ahead of the swelling."

"Later."

"Ice can't wait." I dig through my first aid kit to find an ice pack. "See, this came in handy." With a squeeze, I pop the container, causing the contents to immediately turn cold. I sink down onto the bed next to her to apply the cold pack, making her hiss when it contacts her ankle.

"I just want to rest and forget this day ever happened."

"All of it? I thought some parts of the day were amazing."

"True. It's hard to believe just this morning we were riding bikes and climbing to the top of a lighthouse. It seems like that was ages ago."

I chuckle under my breath. This day was chock-full of surprises. From our time on shore, to LARPing, to Chrissy showing the world that she's as tough as I've always known, this day has been nearly perfect.

She cocks an eyebrow. "What's so funny?"

"This cruise hasn't turned out the way you hoped, huh?"

"Pfft. Stupid magic dust. I found out I do not have the shield of courage."

"I wouldn't go that far."

She smiles. "I did some reading and found out that many 'cruisers' have at least one bad day, but I think I've had my fair share."

"You read too much."

"It has really been the Loathe Boat for sure." She adjusts her leg, which makes her wince. "Ow! That hurts."

"I'm sorry about your ankle." With a deep breath, I blurt out, "I'm sorry about pushing you away and for proposing to you. I clearly did not read the signs that you weren't ready to get married again. And I'm completely and utterly sorry for accusing you about still having feelings for Elliot." I hate bringing up his name right now, but I'm on a roll, and I need to get all my pent-up feelings out there in the open while she's listening to me again.

The silence is deafening, and I'm afraid I've scared her off. We stare at each other for the longest time before she blinks, then she says, "I am sorry about keeping things from you even if it was a surprise for you. From now on, no secrets."

Now would be the right moment to tell her that one tiny piece of my past that I'm not proud of, that I've kept from her. If I phrase it right, she'll understand why I didn't disclose my drinking problems.

But before I can continue, she covers my hand with hers. "I think I need some physical therapy."

Nice! I quirk up an eyebrow. This is going way better than I expected. "What else did you sprain?"

Feeling bold, I slide one hand farther up her thigh. She takes my hand and tugs me toward her until I am on top of her. With my hands cradling her face, we gaze into each other's eyes, nose to nose. I've waited for this moment, and I don't want to do anything to mess it up because I'm so tired of doing this happy-then-angry dance we've been doing this whole time.

Knowing what makes her purr, I kiss the sensitive spot behind her ear, and I'm rewarded with a soft moan that makes me wild. I pull back.

Not wanting to assume anything, I blurt out, "I shouldn't have done that."

"Why not?"

"I don't want to rush things. I tend to get ahead of myself."

She shakes her head. "I think you learned today that I will tell you when you have stepped out of line."

I snort. "You are a warrior. Never let anyone tell you anything different."

"Thank you. I needed to hear that." Her face gets serious again, almost like she's fighting back tears. "Let's get something straight. I've never stopped loving you, not for one second. You hurt me and made me angry, but never enough to hate you, so maybe we can start over."

Her hopeful eyes roam my face as I hover over her. "I would love that. And just so we are completely clear, I am madly in love with you."

I brush my lips to hers. It's the softest feeling in the world, and I've missed her kisses so much. She threads her fingers into my hair, tugging me closer, and I don't want this moment to end. When I move to deepen the kiss, her treacherous stomach growls like an entire circus full of tigers has been unleashed in our stateroom.

Chrissy lets out a breath as I pull back to stare down at her. "Ignore that," she mumbles against my neck, sending my emotions over the edge. She unbuttons my jacket while I fumble with her laced-up corset. "Grishork, my handsome sea demon."

The bed shakes with my rumbling laughter as she pops the last button loose and helps me peel off my jacket. As I hover over her, wearing only my sweaty T-shirt, she slides her hands up my abs and rests them behind my head again. I'll never deserve her, but if she gives me the chance, I will make it my mission to make sure she knows how much I love her.

All in all, tonight might be the best night of the cruise. It's a shame we didn't start out this way. It's probably a good thing it didn't because we wouldn't have left the stateroom the entire time.

Not that I would have complained.

A slip of paper slides under our door, along with a single knock.

"If that's Whitaker…"

Rising from the bed, I let out a groan. "I'll get it." I snatch the paper off the floor and sink back onto the bed next to Chrissy to read it. "It's our disembarkment information. We should be back at Port Miami by three p.m. tomorrow. We are scheduled to disembark at five. We can choose to leave our luggage outside our stateroom to be picked up, or we can lug it down ourselves."

She rests her head on my shoulder and rereads the note. "They can totally pick up my luggage. I'm going down that slide one more time." In a slow, methodical fashion, she rises on one elbow, and her gaze starts at my face and trails down my body then back to my eyes. "You know what this means, right?" When I don't reply, she adds, "We shouldn't waste any more time."

I crumple the paper and toss it onto the floor and wrap my arms around this gorgeous woman. It's hard to believe I almost lost her for good. I'll never do anything to mess things up again.

Chapter Twenty-Two

Deacon

Day Five of the Cruise

Daylight drifts in through the sliding door that leads to the veranda, making me open my eyes. Chrissy's leg drapes over mine as her hand rests on my stomach. I play with a strand of her hair while I wrap my other arm around her shoulders. While I gaze down at her, I wish time could stand still.

We spent the better part of the night making up for lost time, and not even her incessantly growling stomach got in the way of our reconciliation. I've missed how she fits right in the crook of my arm, like she's meant to be there. I've missed the way her hair splays out over the bed, her slow breaths while she sleeps, and even the soft snores that escape her partially open mouth. But nothing beats the sight of when she opens those baby-blue eyes and I'm the first thing she sees.

With a wide yawn, she does that sexy eye flutter thing that makes me weak in the knees. "Good morning sleepyhead." I kiss the top of her head.

She lets out a satisfied sigh that makes my insides turn to mush. "I haven't slept that well since... Well, you make a good pillow." Another cute flush sweeps across her face. She sits up and rubs her ankle. "Sorry I crashed on you."

"You don't hear me complaining."

"You wore me out."

I pull her back to the bed and roll on top of her, careful not to harm her ankle. "I could say the same about you." Remembering the gift I bought her earlier in the week, I add, "I have something for you."

Forcing myself off the bed, I fling on my boxer briefs then scrounge around my drawer until I find what I'm looking for. Now is not the time to pull out the black velvet box, but I retrieve something else that might make her happy. Between my thumb and forefinger, I dangle the charm in the shape of a ship.

Her eyes light up, and she lets out a squeal of delight. "To go on my Pandora bracelet?"

"It's cheesy, but I—"

I don't get to finish my sentence before she pulls me by my shoulders back on top of her. "It's perfect. I love it." She places it on the end table and stares up at me hovering over her. "Can I tell you something?" Her voice is soft and sultry.

I pepper her with kisses. "Not now. I'm kind of busy."

My hands roam her body, and her breath hitches. She closes her eyes and arches her back as my mouth finds that sensitive spot behind her ear.

Channeling my LARPing courage, I clear my throat then say, "I need to tell you something. It's part of my past that I've never mentioned before."

She leans up on her elbow until we're nose to nose. "I'm listening."

It's now or never to come clean. If we're going to have a fresh start, she needs to know everything about me, the good and the bad.

"I'm a recovering alcoholic. I've been sober for over three years, and I know how... *he* treated you when he was drunk, so I was afraid you would think I was that way, and—"

She places a finger on my lips to stop my rambling. "First off, you are not anything like Elliot. Secondly, I already knew."

My eyes fly open as my head snaps back. "You knew?"

"I found a sobriety coin in the washer a while ago. It must have fallen out of your pocket when you did your laundry. I figured you would tell me when and if you wanted to." She rolls over and places a hand on each side of my face, so I have no choice but to gaze into her beautiful eyes. "I'm proud of you for getting sober. That's not easy."

I hug the life out of her and whisper into her neck, "Thank you." I truly do not deserve this woman. With all my heart, I wish I could propose right now, but I have to know that she's definitely on board, and we aren't completely there yet.

"One more confession."

She leans back to put some space between us, her eyebrow cocked up in an incredulous fashion. "I'm listening."

I gulp, take a breath, and blurt it out before I can talk myself out of it. "Angela recently got out of rehab, and I'm her sponsor."

Chrissy's expression doesn't change, but I can almost see her brain cells processing this extra piece of information. She nods one slow time then replies, "I did not see that coming, but I guess I can appreciate you want her to be clean also."

"I promise you with every fiber of my being: I do not want to get back with Angela. I'm not in love with her."

She chews on her bottom lip then snickers. "The Sea Demon did profess his undying love for me in the duel."

I crack a grin. "Yes, I, er... he did."

She yawns as she snuggles into me. "I believe you."

"Why did I let you go?" I mumble in her ear.

"I didn't go. You did, but I understand why. My reaction to your proposal was less than stellar." Her arms slide around my waist then up my chest, and I feel like I've finally come home, being here with her.

"But I didn't let you explain, so I was a jerk. Please give this idiot another chance. Chrissy, I love you so much." If she doesn't, I don't know what I'll do. I've loved her since the first day I laid eyes on her, and she was never shy about telling me how she felt, but that was before the failed proposal.

"I love you too. I never stopped."

As I lie on top of her, we kiss more, making up for lost time. I enjoy the feel of her body pressed against mine, her hands holding me tight like she never wants to let go. We may not see the sky or do the Flowrider one more time, but this last full day of our cruise will be one for the books. She lets out a satisfied smile as I plant a kiss on the tip of her nose, and I never want to leave.

"Definitely the flippy-floppies."

I couldn't agree more.

Chapter Twenty-Three

Chrissy

We lie in the bed, tangled up in the sheets as we soak up the moment. Neither of us seems to be in any hurry to get up and get dressed to start the day. I wish we'd done this on day one, because the cruise would've been so much better. Way better.

Deacon plays with my hair as I draw circles on his bare chest, and I never want to leave this place. Maybe we can stow away and live like vagabonds on the ship. I could get a job as a yoga instructor or run a kiosk booth selling friendship rings. Deacon could take care of the injuries of the passengers. Nothing would make me happier, especially if he's by my side.

"I just realized something."

Still playing with my hair, he asks, "What's that?"

"I finally got to sleep in the bed."

Deacon snickers. "Yeah, I'm not proud of how I stole it from you."

"You didn't steal anything. Rock, paper, scissors is legally binding."

He clears his throat. I glance up to see his eyes twinkle. "In case you haven't already figured it out, there is a black velvet box in the drawer with your name on it."

I wiggle as I smile, assuming where he's going with this. "Are you going to ask to be my... friend again?"

He chuckles, making my head bounce off his chest, and oh, I've missed that chest. "Not exactly. Do you know where I'm going with this?"

"I hope so, but don't do it today."

His arm muscles tense around me. "Why?"

"Because thirty-seven percent of couples who get engaged on an extravagant vacation don't make it to their second anniversary."

He rolls over until he's on top then peppers every inch of my face with kisses. "I've missed you and your incessant stats."

"I've missed you too. Even your obsession with the cycle of obesity."

"I promise to do my best to tone that down. Gotta live a little, am I right?"

My jaw drops open, which makes him tickle my side. "What have you done with my Deacon? Is this Grishork the Sea Demon speaking?"

His eyebrows dance. "I'll never tell. What do you want to do on our last day of the cruise?" By the way his eyebrows dance, I know where his mind has gone. Mine has too, but we need to take advantage of what the ship has to offer, other than a place for second chances. "As much fun as that *may* be..."

"May?"

I give him a warning glance. "The LARPers are having a festival to celebrate the end of the cruise and to welcome us to the Land of Fruitful Earth or something like that."

His entire body shakes from laughter.

"Their gathering sounds like fun. You can wear that sexy sea demon jacket again." Now, I'm the one waggling *my* brows. "And don't worry about anything. I'm not going to freak out on you again. I'm not going anywhere."

Every nerve in my body activates when his lips touch mine. My hands roam up his back, then he pulls away.

"Are you sure about the festival? Your words say you want to go, but your body is speaking a totally different and extremely appealing language."

With a playful shove, I nudge him off me. "Yes. Plus, I'm hungry."

"There's a shocker."

He rises from the bed and holds out a hand to me then leads me to the bathroom, where we find out the fun way how small the shower really is—totally worth being cramped.

For the next thirty minutes, we go between getting dressed and making out. We get distracted by the slightest brush of a hand. Even putting on makeup turns into a kissing session.

After another searing kiss, we force ourselves out into the real world in search of food, because I have seriously worked up an appetite now. Even with other guests in the elevator, nothing stops Deacon's hands from being all over me, not that I'm putting up a fight.

When the elevator pings and the doors open to the promenade deck, the girl in the elevator with us shoves past, saying over her shoulder, "Gross."

We fall out of the elevator in a fit of laughter. Coming straight toward us is Elliot. He stomps so hard with each footstep that he might punch holes in the floor. With fire in his eyes, he marches up to me.

What does he want this time?

"Did you forget to tell her about something?" His eyes are slits as he stands there, nose to nose with Deacon, tapping a toe. "If you don't tell her, I will."

"What are you talking about?" I stare at Elliot until he takes a step away from Deacon.

"Tell Chrissy about your little stowaway."

Deacon flinches as the blood drains from his face.

With clenched jaw, he stares at Elliot, who has a cocky grin on his face, one that I'd love nothing better than to smack right now.

With hands on my fists, I say, "I do not know what you are trying to pull, but you need to back off."

The sound of hurried footsteps quickly approaching interrupts my words. An all-too-familiar feminine voice yells, "Elliot, what are you doing?"

My neck hurts from how fast I whip around to see Angela standing there. Her black-and-purple hair, pulled into a high ponytail, swishes around her neck. I feel like she punched me in the chest and all the wind is knocked out of me. Her frantic expression can't be anything compared to how mine must be.

"Angela?" In slow motion, I turn to Deacon. "Did you know she was on board?"

He closes his eyes and blows out a breath, and when he opens them again, I know with one hundred percent certainty that he knew.

"Yes, but..." He glares at her and adds through gritted teeth, "I told you to stay in your cabin."

My head spins as I process this horrific scene. Tears pool in my eyes as I back up against the wall. He and his ex are here together, and I guess I was just a big joke to them.

My throat is dry, but I finally eke out, "You lied. Everything was a lie."

He shakes his head with so much force that he's going to knock something loose if I don't do it first. "No. Nothing was a lie, at least from my point of view. If you'll let me explain. Please."

He reaches out to touch my arm, but I jerk it out of his grip. "Don't touch me. I can't believe I was finally ready to accept your proposal, and now this."

Elliot steps toward me. "Sweetheart, let's go talk."

"No! I don't know what you're up to, but neither of you are worth it. Just go away."

A flash of anger crosses Elliot's face, then it's replaced by pain. His shoulders slump as he stares at the ground. I guess he thought he would spill the beans and swoop in to be my savior. But I don't need him to be my knight in shining armor. I can save myself.

Angela stands there, covering her mouth with her hands as she stares at Elliot then us.

Deacon motions in the direction of Elliot's retreating frame and tells me, "He's not telling you the entire truth. I can explain everything."

Imitating his action, I motion toward Angela, who leans against the wall and looks like she's about to hyperventilate. "Am I supposed to believe her being here is a silly coincidence?" I hate using air quotes, but it gives my flailing arms something to do.

"No. It's not a coincidence, but please let me explain."

"He's telling the truth," Angela squeaks out. "I promise I'm not here to cause trouble. If you would just let me clarify everything."

I scoff. "No one wants to hear from you. As much fun as it sounds, I think I can fill in all the missing pieces on my own."

Deacon holds up a hand for me to stop talking. He shakes his head as he stares at the floor. Mumbling something to himself, he backs up and walks down the hallway. "It's completely obvious now that it was a mistake to go on this cruise."

My mouth opens and closes, but no words come out. Deacon turns back to stare at me for what seems like an eternity. He swallows hard, his Adam's apple bobbing as tears pool in his eyes. "I love you, Chrissy, but I guess it's not enough if you don't trust me."

I've never seen him this close to tears, and something inside me cracks. He scrubs his face with his hands as he walks away, head hanging low.

Angela's gaze ping-pongs between me and Deacon like she can't decide whether to stay put or to follow him. Finally, she says, "I'll be right back. Don't go anywhere."

"We're on a ship in the middle of the ocean, you dingbat. Where do you think I'm going?"

She holds her hands out in defense, like she's trying to talk me down from jumping off a cliff. "That is a valid point. I'm just going to say this last comment, and you can take it or leave it. You have it all wrong. I don't want him. He doesn't want me." She throws her hands in the air and runs in the direction Deacon went as I slide down the wall and hold my head in my hands to start a massive crying jag.

From the other direction, Charmaine flits down the hallway, all dressed in her elf costume, chatting with her LARP friends. When she sees me crumpled in a heap, her smile fades. "What happened?"

I wipe tears from my face, and through shaking breaths, I say, "I'm working on my backstory and it's really, really sad."

"Honey, you're doing it all wrong."

She helps me to my feet and escorts me back to my stateroom. When I open the door, she oohs and ahhs over the place. "This is much nicer than mine." When she spots the veranda, she gasps. "You have your own deck? Get your booty out here right now." She pushes me outside and plunks me into one of the lounge chairs, and the salty air whips around my face as the sun shines in my eyes.

We sit out on the veranda for what seems like hours, doing nothing but watching seagulls flit around and the waves crash into the side of the ship. Charmaine orders us drinks, but I'm not in the mood, so she slurps them all down.

After I catch her up with all the drama, she tsks. "Men."

"I agree."

"The most honest men I know dress as elves and warlords. Is that pathetic?" Her words make me chuckle as she takes the last sip of her drink. "Take it from an old gal like me: men flee at the first mention of commitment."

"In this case, it was me being wishy-washy. Deacon was all in, or so I thought. Can you believe he had his ex on the ship all this time?"

She runs her finger around the rim of her glass as she stares off toward the sea. "But your ex was here too. That's kind of sketchy."

"That's different."

"How so?"

"Because I don't have feelings for Elliot."

She frowns at her empty glass. "And how is that different from Deacon's ex if you don't know the whole story?"

With shock, I sit up abruptly and stare at her. "He chose to keep it from me." I pound the heel of my hand into my forehead. "I'm so stupid."

"Yep."

My jaw drops. "Thanks for agreeing."

She winks, so I know she heard my sarcasm. "You are stupid, but not for that reason."

If I sit here long enough, maybe some wisdom will come to me. None of my fortune cookies are helping me on this one, and nothing in the LARP NPC handbook is likely to tell me what to do, so I'm on my own. Resting my head back on my lounge chair, I let out a deep, defeated sigh while I spin the friendship ring around on my finger. "All I know is that I can't wait to get off this ship and forget this cruise ever happened."

I haven't updated April, and I really need her advice, so I pull up WhatsApp.

Her smiling face morphs into a frown when she sees my bloodshot, puffy eyes. "What happened?"

After I catch her up on all the drama, she pretty much reiterates what Charmaine said, which makes Charmaine say, "I told ya."

"Who is that?" April scrunches her brow.

"It's a friend I made on board."

"Hey," Charmaine says, waving at the screen.

April waves back. "Hey, Auntie Lucky."

My head spins as I rewind the last minute of this conversation. *Auntie Lucky?* "You two know each other?"

Charmaine nods with a coy wink. "April is my faux niece. Her mom and I go way back."

"She went from being called Charmaine to Lucky Charm to Auntie Lucky. Isn't she a peach?"

My jaw drops as I process her words. "How? What? I... don't understand."

Charmaine pats my hand. "April was worried about you and told me about the crazy cruise you were going on. She wanted me to keep an eye on you and maybe help you and Deacon get back together. I'm sorry that didn't happen."

"Don't be mad," April says. "I did it because I care about you and think you and Deacon are meant to be together. Call me tomorrow when you get home, and we'll eat ice cream and watch sappy movies, okay?"

I swipe a tear from my face as I nod and say goodbye. To Charmaine, I say, "She's the best friend anyone could ask for."

With a gentle pat on my hand, Charmaine says, "It will all work out, sugar. I know it will. Just trust me."

No amount of fairy dust on this ship can make me feel better. I'm just going to hide in my cabin until we disembark. We can't dock soon enough.

Chapter Twenty-Four

My brain hasn't caught up with the fact that everything came to a boil this morning. The high I was riding from reconciling with Chrissy came to a disastrous crash when Whitaker had to get the last word and tell Chrissy that Angela was on board. I know I should've told her myself, but lately, I am my own worst enemy.

For the second time in my life, I was ready to propose because I was so confident we were on the same page and I wasn't jumping the gun this time. But he swooped in and spilled the beans before I had a chance. That was a jerk move, even for him.

"Dea!" Angela screams through the ship as her footsteps stomp toward me. "Stop."

Not. Happening. "I don't want to talk to you right now."

Angela screeches to a halt in front of me, her hair looks like a rat's nest, and I don't think I've ever seen her run, so at least that part is amusing. When she pulls up to me, she leans over to catch her breath.

"You are a fast walker."

"Torture does that to a guy."

"I'm sorry I exposed myself to her, but I was having breakfast with Elliot, and he told me—"

"Wait. You were eating with Whitaker?" *What is it with this guy that all my exes gravitate toward him?*

She acts like she's going to choke me, and I may just let her so that I can be put out of my misery. "That's not important right now. What is urgent is that he told me he was so mad that she rejected him that he was going to make her pay. The best way to punish you was to reveal I was on the ship. If he couldn't have her, you couldn't either. His words. I'm not lying."

"I don't care. He just wants to impress you. Why, I'll never know."

A flash of hurt crosses her face, but it quickly morphs into a fit of fire that I remember all too well. She throws her shoulders back and takes me by the arm. "You need to calm down. Let's go back to my state-room so you can work out your frustrations."

Oh no, she didn't say that. I snap my head back, hoping I didn't hear her correctly. "Excuse me?"

She sneers as she tugs me toward the stairwell. "That is not what I meant. Gah, you're such a guy."

She drags me down two more flights of steps and down a long corridor then opens the door to wave me in. Her cabin is super cramped with two twin beds, a small monitor, and not even a window. It isn't even as big as a dorm room. A rolled-up yoga mat is propped in a corner, along with some stretchy bands.

When I sink down onto the bed that appears to be her extra closet space, I say, "Now, I see why you're so eager to get out of this eight-by-ten box."

"Yeah, this is what you get when you're staff. I'm right above the nightclub, so I listen to that all night long. Lucky for me, I did convince my brother to let me take his PlayStation with me, so it hasn't been all bad."

My knees buckle when I see the shiny new PS5 system. "Call of Duty, Grand Theft Auto..." I pick up one game and quirk up an eyebrow. "Final Fantasy VII?"

She snatches it out of my hand. "And it's been a great tutorial for LARPing. You should try it sometime."

"I did LARP yesterday and came close to beating the crap out of Elliot."

Angela chuckles. "I wish I'd been a fly on the wall for that one. Did you punch him?"

"They have rules. No hitting the head, which I think is really stupid, especially when it's him."

She flops onto the other twin bed and turns on the device, and a game called Sonic Superstars pops up on the small screen. When I don't say anything, she says, "It was already in the system, so I assume it's my brother's favorite. It's actually not bad at all. I will play as Amy Rose, and you can play as Miles Prower." When I don't move, she adds, "Come on. I promise it will make you feel better."

"Fine." If it will stop her yapping, I'll do just about anything at this point because I don't want to talk about anything that happened this morning.

She tosses me a controller and starts the game. As much as I hate to admit it, she's right about Sonic Superstars. After fifteen minutes, my stiff muscles are starting to relax even if I still feel like crap. Angela sticks her tongue out as she jerks around like she's helping her character jump and run.

"Boom." She pumps her fist in the air as she wins a round.

I let the controller slip out of my hand as I hold out a fist for her to bump.

"Feel better?"

"No. Maybe a little."

She rotates to focus on me while I slump on the bed. "Tell me everything."

"We had such a great night making up, then Whitaker had to ruin everything this morning. It's not all his fault. He took a nugget of information and used it to his advantage. It could have all been avoided had I told Chrissy you were here. She would have flipped out, but the truth wouldn't have been used against me by him."

For a moment, we sit in silence. She picks up the stretchy band and holds it over her head then pulls the ends down and away from her body, completing a set of lat pull downs. "But aren't you going to try to tell her your side of the story?"

I shrug, making her groan.

Smacking my arm with the stretchy band, she huffs. "Deacon, you are so stubborn. Now, I remember why we didn't work out. The only thing you were good for was to encourage me to be sober."

"How's that working?" I hope that after all this, that hasn't been a disaster, at least.

She gazes off and blows out a breath. "It's hard, especially when I'm surrounded by alcohol at every turn, but I need to stay sober. I don't think I've thanked you enough for being my sponsor. I owe you big time, and I am so sorry things happened like they did. And to think I was one day from being off the ship without being found out."

"You don't owe me anything."

"If it makes you feel better, I did find someone else to be my sponsor, so you're off the hook from now on."

"If that's what you want." I shove her clothes out of the way and lie back on the bed. "Wake me up when it's time to get off this ship."

"Gah. You are so stubborn. Don't you want to fight for her?" She hovers over me with her hands on her hips.

"No. She doesn't trust me."

She nudges my foot. "Not to take Elliot's side, but you should've said something to her before now."

"Don't you think I already know that? But it would've only made things worse."

With her hands on her hips, she stares down at me. "There's a *worse* than what you have right now?"

"Go away. You're bothering me. Just let me wallow in my suffering." I throw one forearm over my eyes, hoping she'll get the hint to leave me alone. "I mess things up at every turn. I guess it's not meant to be with Chrissy."

She *fwops* me with a pillow. "You're impossible."

"I've been called worse."

"Ugh. You're impossible."

"You said that already." If I tick her off enough, she'll get the hint I don't want to be bothered. All I want to do is have a pity party all by myself without her chirping in my ear. I know this is her cabin, but I have no place else to go. I just want to hide out until I see Miami again.

After another swipe with the pillow, she lets out an exasperated groan. "I'm out of here. Now that the cat is out of the bag, I don't have to stick around in this third-class cabin. Have fun being a butthead."

With that parting insult, she slams the door behind herself, leaving me in her room alone. Thank goodness, it's finally quiet in my head, with nothing except this morning's events, which won't stop playing on a loop. I'm tired of her incessant nagging. Through all the internal chatter, I'm left with her words, "fight for her," in my head.

Should I?

Love shouldn't be this hard. If it was meant to be, Chrissy and I would've used this cruise as an engagement celebration, but other than the amazing morning we were having, this cruise has definitely not been anything worthy of partying about. My stomach rumbles, but I don't care. I'd rather lie here and stew over my sucky love life than go in search of food. And another round of Sonic Superstars wouldn't hurt anything. I start it up again, becoming a believer that this is one of the best PlayStation games ever. No one can convince me otherwise.

I just wish I could start this day all over and tell Chrissy everything. She was so understanding when I came clean about my problems with alcohol—I could have segued right into telling her Angela was here, but I was terrified I would mess things up. Boy, did I mess things up big time.

That doesn't stop me from trying to contact Chrissy. She's not picking up. I text, call—which is pointless out here on the ocean—and WhatsApp, but she's not having any of it because she's done with me.

I really, really miss her, but I saw the way she looked at me, like nothing was left in her heart for us. And I don't blame her.

Chapter Twenty-Five

Chrissy

Charmaine and I fall into a comfortable silence. On her part, it's probably the booze, but for me, it's her incessant yammering on about her new LARPing friends. She has definitely had more fun this week than I have. She's totally into it and signed up to be a part of her local LARPing community. And the fact that April sent her here to watch over me warms my soul. Thinking back, Charmaine seemed to be around every corner, and now, it all makes sense.

Also, I'm just all talked out. My brain is fuzzy from everything that happened this morning, but my heart feels like someone stuck a knife in my chest and twisted it. I'm so tired and all cried out that I just stare off into the ocean, not caring that Deacon has tried to contact me at least five times in the last hour.

Right when I'm about to doze off to sleep on my very comfy veranda, someone bangs on my stateroom door, startling me. I flail my arms, knocking Charmaine's glass off the table next to me.

My heart thumps in my chest, and I'm afraid it will explode. "If that's Deacon, he can wait until later this afternoon to get his things when I'm packed and gone."

Saying his name starts another tsunami of tears again. So much for being all cried out, because I can't swipe them away fast enough. I'm mad, sad, and every emotion in between.

Charmaine rises and says, "I'll see who it is."

I wipe my face and force myself to stare out at the waves, pretending not to care who is at the door. A hushed conversation behind me piques my interest, but not enough to move. It doesn't sound like Deacon, and if it's Elliot, I don't want to know. Elliot has never been good at getting the hint, but even he should know better than to come near me right now, if he knows what's good for him.

"Uh, honey, you have a visitor." Charmaine squeezes my shoulder.

"If that no-good two-timer—" My words die in my mouth when Angela appears next to me, nibbling on a fingernail. Slow as a snail, I rise from my chair and take a step toward her. "What do you want? To rub it in that you won?"

Angela glances around my stateroom and whistles. "Dang. This is nice. You should see my cabin." She does a full-body shiver. "I don't even have a window."

With a wave of her hand, like she's Vanna White, Charmaine says, "You should check out the view."

"Excuse me, ladies. If you are finished..." My words come out a bit snippier than I intended, but these two women are driving me crazy.

Angela glances over to Charmaine. "Is she always this petulant?"

Charmaine holds out her hands in a defensive gesture. "Beats me. I just met her a few days ago, but my faux niece thought she needed a fairy godmother onboard, so here I am."

My nemesis clutches her chest and says, "Aw, that is so sweet."

"I've tried to get her to go to the LARP festival at noon, but she won't budge out of that chair." In a stage whisper, she adds, "She could really use a makeover too."

My jaw drops open. "Harsh. I think I've earned my haggard appearance. Don't you agree?"

"It's the puffy red eyes." Angela sticks a finger out to touch my face, but I swat it away.

Charmaine agrees with Angela then adds, "She needs a massage. Ooh. Let's do that. Girl time."

Angela and Charmaine do a happy dance then swallow their excitement when they see me sneering.

"Angela, what could you possibly want? You have taken my boyfriend. You've invaded my cruise. If you try to take my stateroom, I may push you overboard."

She takes me by the arm to lead me to the sofa, but I yank away. She holds her hands out in defense and backs off. "Okay, I won't touch you, but you need to listen to me. I come in peace."

Crossing my arms over my chest, I sink down onto the sofa with a huff. "I don't have to listen to you or do anything."

"You do if you want to win Deacon back." She leans over me and stabs me in the chest with her index finger, but I smack it away. "You still love him." Angela accentuates each word with a poke, poke, poke to my chest.

"That's rich coming from you, you... homewrecker."

She throws her hands in the air and lets out a groan. "I am not a homewrecker."

"What would you call it? Seductress? Temptress? Casanova?"

Angela snorts then sits next to me on the couch as Charmaine lurks in the corner, appearing as uncomfortable as I feel. I scoot an inch away from Angela to make sure she gets that I don't want her here.

"Deacon adores you. A blind man can see it."

"Pfft."

With her hands balled into fists, she says, "You are both so stubborn and pigheaded. Do you know why I am here?"

For emphasis, I count on my fingers. "To gloat, to rub it in my face that he's in love with you, or maybe just to make me miserable. Can it be all the above? Right now, it really doesn't matter." I bite my lip to keep it from trembling.

Angela closes her eyes and mumbles something under her breath. It sounds like part of the Serenity Prayer. When she opens her eyes, her expression changes from frustration to concern. "I'm in your stateroom trying to knock some sense into you. But the reason I'm on the ship is because..."

"The suspense is killing me." My deadpan tone makes her roll her eyes.

"I'm an alcoholic, and Deacon is my sponsor. I just got out of rehab, and I was terrified if I wasn't within earshot of him, I'd slip up, and I really, really don't want to relapse. It was my idea to be here, and he didn't want you to know because he was afraid you'd get the wrong idea, which is exactly what happened when you found out."

Her words sink in. He told me pretty much the same thing earlier about being her sponsor, but he didn't mention her being on this ship.

"While I respect what you're going through and glad that you chose to get sober, couldn't you just call him if you felt the urge to drink?"

"In the middle of the ocean? And don't tell me you wouldn't have minded if I FaceTimed him. I thought the ship was so big we'd never run into each other, and we made it five days without that happening, so my plan almost worked. If it weren't for that vindictive ex-husband of yours..." She lets out a chuckle and stares at the ceiling. "I was beginning to like the guy. We had breakfast, and he was funny and sweet, but then I realized his motive, which was to drive a wedge between you and Deacon."

"That about sums up the entirety of Elliot."

Charmaine sinks down beside me on the sofa, so I'm sandwiched between two women acting like this is an intervention. I'm ready to hear the "You hurt me in the following ways" lecture, but I'm the one who should be making that speech and not either one of them.

"I can vouch for Angela," Charmaine says. "She's been hiding. We bonded over the slot machines. She's not after your man."

"He's not *my* man," I grind out.

Standing up to pace around the room as I chew on a fingernail, I let this new information sink in. I never led Elliot on, or at least I hoped I never did. Even when Deacon and I were apart, I don't think I ever implied that I wanted him back in *that* capacity.

Did I? I hope not.

"Deacon should have trusted me enough to tell me everything."

Angela cocks her head to the side at my constant stubbornness. She mulls over my words while my head pounds with all the stress of the day.

"Wait!" Charmaine says, interrupting my thoughts. "Elliot is your ex-boyfriend?"

I wince. "Worse. He's my ex-husband."

Charmaine's mouth forms a large *O* as she processes. "I did not see that one coming."

"But we're better off as friends."

Angela chuckles. "Says no guy ever. But forget Elliot. Deacon loves you. Really loves you. He only kept the fact that I was here under wraps because he wanted to win you back. If you knew I was here, you would never have believed him."

My fairy godmother holds up a finger to interject her opinion. "And putting all that aside, Deacon is *H. O. T.* Hot. I have never seen a sexier sea demon. That costume was yummy. Who am I kidding? He'd be a tasty snack in a croker sack." Charmaine blushes as she fans her face, and I have to stifle a smile.

While I review what Angela told me, I blow out a breath. Maybe everything with Deacon and Angela was as innocent as she says. It must be, or she wouldn't be here right now trying to set the record straight. We've never been friends, but for some reason I think I believe her.

"I miss Deacon so much. If I had just accepted his proposal months ago, none of this would have happened."

"What is wrong with you?" Charmaine teases as she pops me on the shoulder. "I'm kidding. I've had so many proposals. Ed at the bar expressed his undying love to me while wielding a foam sword just last night, but it didn't feel right. You know what I mean?"

I peek over at Angela, who hides a grin behind her hand.

"I do know what you mean. I loved Deacon enough to marry him, but I didn't want to mess it up. I already have one failed marriage. It would be totally humiliating to have two before I'm thirty."

"Try four ex-husbands." Charmaine checks her nails as if her statement is as commonplace as what flavor of coffee she prefers.

"What?" Angela screeches. When I pop her on the arm, she clears her throat. "What I mean is that's so sad."

Good save, Ange.

Charmaine stares off toward the ocean. "I don't want to leave this ship."

"I'm not," Angela proclaims. She spreads her arms wide and adds, "You are looking at the new fitness director of the *Sovereign of the Seas*. I'm flying back to Nashville to pack up, and I set sail again in a week. It won't be a LARPing cruise, which is strangely disappointing, but I am stoked about this opportunity."

My mouth drops open as I process her words. "That's amazing. Not to put a damper on your news, but won't you need a sponsor nearby?"

She winks. "I've already taken care of that. The cruise director agreed to take over Deacon's role. I am so excited." By the way she bounces and claps like a cheerleader, her enthusiasm is evident.

Angela jerks to a standing position and bounces on her toes. "I have a great idea."

"No."

She huffs and plants her hands on her hips. "You haven't even heard it yet. Where is that sea demon costume?"

I wave a hand toward the closet. "I assume it's in there."

She rummages around in the closet, making clothes hangers fly across the room. "Got it. Okay, I'll get Deacon to the festival. You get Elliot there."

Surely, she didn't just say that. I point at myself as my brain tries to keep up with her crazy talk. "Me? Why?"

"Yeah. Convince him you want to reconcile."

Nope. No way. "But I don't."

With a wicked grin, Angela says, "Exactly, but he does need to pay for what he did. Charmaine, do you think your LARP friends could help us out?"

"Absolutely." She rubs her hands together like she's already planning the deed.

"What's going on here?" I stare from Angela to Charmaine. "I think I should just discuss it with Elliot at some other time when my emotions have had a chance to settle. I certainly don't want to lead him on. Obviously, that's very easy to do."

Charmaine smacks her forehead. "I just remembered something, and this might change your mind. Elliot was hanging out at the bar one night. He'd had a few too many drinks, and I wasn't sure what he was talking about at the time, but I bet you will. During his diatribe, he said he put a sock on someone's door. I just passed it off as maybe he was being a neat freak and saw it lying in the hallway. Could it be something important? Does that mean anything to you?"

Oh. My. Gosh. I suck in all the air in the room. "You're kidding me."

All this time, I thought the sock on the doorknob meant Deacon was hooking up with that Monique girl. He kept telling me he didn't know what I was talking about, and now it makes sense. But it was Elliot who did it, just to put a wedge between me and Deacon. He's a low-down rat fink jerk-face. And I bet he assumed I would ask if I could stay the night in his room. Thank goodness I didn't fall for it.

Angela and Charmaine shake hands as if they understand what's going on. Angela grins at me. "You are going to win your man back. That is, if you still want him."

Do I?

Imagining my life without Deacon is painful. I want to grow old with him. Have babies with him. Expand my fortune-writing career into greeting cards. I want a forever with him. My answer is absolutely obvious. Instead of answering, I hug Angela, my former enemy and new friend. I'm going to win my man back and make my ex pay.

For one last time, I slip on my wench costume. Something about this garb gives me more confidence than usual. I hope this works. This had better work.

Standing in front of Elliot's door, I blow out a breath before I knock. When he opens the door, his eyes grow big as he gazes at my wench costume.

"Chrissy. I'm so glad you're here." He wraps his arms around me in a big hug and even though I don't want to hug him back, I have to in order to make this as convincing as possible. "How are you doing? Let me explain." He ushers me into his room.

"It's okay. No need. I kind of thought it was sweet that you were willing to fight for me like that. You were so kind." *Blech. I can't believe I said that with a straight face.*

He plants his hands on my shoulders and stares into my eyes. "I should have fought harder for you before. It's been agonizing just being your friend, but you have no idea how painful it's been to see you and Deacon together. When you broke up, I was elated. And then you were going on a cruise with him anyway... Well, I had to do something."

"Shh. Don't worry about it. The fact that Angela was on board too was the nail in the coffin, so to speak. It's just too much to process."

"Shall I order some lunch? We can talk, and I promise we'll take it slow this time. I don't want to rush you at all."

And he thinks I believe him...

I pause as I gain the courage I need in order to continue. "I want to do something fun today. Do you still have your LARP costume?"

He cracks a grin and motions with his head toward the closet. "Want to role-play?"

Gross.

"Sort of. The LARPers are having an end-of-the-cruise festival. I really want to go, but not by myself. Do you want to accompany me? We can come back here and... talk later."

I can almost see the wheels turning in his head. He grins again and says, "What the heck? Let's do it. One last hurrah, right?"

Absolutely.

Chapter Twenty-Six

It's a good thing Angela is a snacker, or I would be starving by now. I'm too depressed to leave her cabin in search of food, so I put a major dent in her snack stash. I've consumed three power bars, two bottles of Gatorade, and an entire bag of Doritos while playing video games. I've made it to the Egg Fortress Zone, Act Two, so I'm totally stoked. At least it took the edge off my crappy week. If Chrissy could see me now, she would get a kick out of me eating all this junk food.

Thoughts of Chrissy turn my stomach and mood sour again. I can't believe how everything turned upside down this morning. I was so ready to propose to her again, but I guess I'm glad I didn't get rejected. Again.

Angela is probably out there, having a great time on the last day at sea. She deserves it after being stuck inside this tiny room the whole time. At least she's having fun. I am so ready to be back home and forget this cruise ever happened. Nothing turned out like I hoped. One star. Would not recommend.

Like a tornado, Angela blasts into the room, carrying a bag from one of the restaurants and a jacket draped over her shoulder. She sees the empty snack bags littering the floor and scoffs. "I guess you don't need food since you found my inventory."

She plunks down the food bag and throws the jacket at me.

"What is this?"

"That is your sea demon costume. Put it on."

"No."

"Yes. We are going to have some fun even if it kills you. There is this awesome last-day event happening with the LARPers. It's supposed to be super cool, and we are going."

"I don't feel like celebrating."

"Come on." She pouts as she stomps her foot on the floor. "Live a little. You're single, right? Maybe you'll find your true love with an elf or fairy."

And that's supposed to make me change my mind? "No way. As much fun as that sounds, I think I'll pass."

She points at the jacket. "Put that on, and I'm not taking no for an answer. I'm going into the bathroom to change into my wizard costume. When I get back, you'd better be ready to party." She lets out a "whoop whoop," and I roll my eyes. She's like the Energizer bunny, with her unlimited endurance.

I stare at the stupid jacket and resign myself to the fact that I should just put it on and go with Angela because she will never shut up if I don't. Maybe some fresh air would do me some good. Besides, the walls of this tiny cabin are closing in on me.

With the jacket on, I pull out the do-rag from the pocket. When it's secured on my head, I blow out a breath. For the next hour, I'm no longer Deacon. I'm Grishork, the Sea Demon, the creature who needs someone to save *him* this time.

When Angela reappears from the bathroom, she eyes me and claps. "That's the spirit. Let's go." She grabs me by the arm and drags me down the hallway and up to the sun deck.

As soon as we get off the elevator, the medieval music wafts over me. The entire section of the ship is transformed into a castle, including a drawbridge over a moat filled with blue plastic balls, which I assume is supposed to mimic water. Fairies flit around, spreading their magic—I could use some magic right about now. No battles seem to be happening today, so hopefully, no one will die any amounts of death. A bunch of LARPers stand in line to take selfies with a massive dragon situated in one corner.

Angela squeals when she sees some of her new friends acting out their characters. A nymph offers me a goblet, but I wave her off. On a day like today, I have to stay strong and not be tempted to drink any alcohol.

Out of the corner of my eye, I see Chrissy enter. My mouth waters as I see her saunter in wearing her sexy wench costume. The cinched waist and low-cut blouse accentuate her breasts. She has a quiver full of foam arrows strapped to her back, and even though I should be revolted at the sight of her, seeing her makes me miss her even more until—

What?

My enthusiasm fades when I see who's standing next to her in his garb minus the face mask. Elliot Whitaker's smarmy, smug expression grows bigger when we lock eyes, like he's taunting me. He snakes a hand around Chrissy's shoulders, and I just can't stomach watching. As bile rises in my throat, I storm away toward the entrance, but Angela blocks my exit.

"Ange, don't get in my way. I can't deal with them today. Did you know they were going to be here?"

She pleads with her eyes as her nails dig into my arm. "Just watch. I promise you'll thank me later."

Charmaine is at the entrance of the castle and wolf whistles to get everyone's attention. "Hey y'all, the Crowned Prince of the *Sovereign of the Sea* has an important announcement to make."

All the guests quiet down as everyone focuses on a man wearing a regal cloak, stepping forward. Not a sound can be heard except for the waves sloshing against the ship.

"It has come to my attention that a serious infraction has been committed."

People take up hushed conversations about what it could be. Angela walks up to Chrissy and gives her a side hug. I shake my head to make sure I'm really witnessing this. I have seriously been transported to another time when my exes are buddy-buddy. *Spitting venom.*

"Elliot Whitaker, can you step forward, please?"

The crowd glances around until their gazes land on Elliot, who has lost all color in his face. Like a game show model, Chrissy waves him toward the prince. Tentatively, he walks toward the guy, looking back at Angela and Chrissy as they blow him patronizing kisses.

"Did you intentionally mislead Chrissy Parks into thinking her cabinmate had a sexual encounter in their stateroom?"

My brain is playing catch-up until I remember the incident in question. Chrissy kept asking me about a sock. He must have put one on the door to make her think I was hooking up with someone. He's the worst kind of jerk because while he's pleasant to one's face, he's stabbing them in the back.

He blinks and snaps his head toward Chrissy, but she doesn't appear to be ready to help him out of the situation. "Uh... you see, I think there's been a little misunderstanding."

"Answer the question!" the man yells, and I swear Elliot shrinks about three inches.

"Er, yes." He glances around and lets out a nervous chuckle like none of this is real anyway, so it doesn't matter.

The crowd begins to mumble to one another until yells come from various parts of the deck.

"Treason!"

"Boo!"

"Guilty!"

The LARPers are very vocal about how they disapprove of his actions. I am loving this a bit too much, especially since he looks scared enough to pee his pants.

"I can explain," he says.

More guests boo him and give him the thumbs-down. Angela and Chrissy join in the chanting, but my brain is still catching up to the fact that the two of them have apparently set him up.

The prince yanks him by the arm and shoves him into a makeshift jail cell made of PVC pipes. His knuckles are white as he clings to the pipes like he's in a real jail.

"I hereby announce you are guilty of treacherous acts against a lady."

The LARPers whoop at the news and start up a song about being merry and grand, and I think it's kind of fitting. It's also very hilarious that Elliot yells, "Nooooooo!" like this infraction is really going to be added to a police record and that Mr. Parks would not approve. Maybe they will keep him in that makeshift jail until we dock.

Chrissy sashays over to me, looking amazing in her skimpy costume. I only hope she's not going to use those arrows on me. I deserve it if she does take aim.

Stopping a foot away, she says, "Hey." Her breathless voice sinks into my soul. I miss it so much even though it's only been a few hours since we last spoke.

"Hello." I bow low and wink. "Is it Chrissy or Calico?"

A grin spreads across her face. "Either one works. But I am a fortune teller or a fortune cookie writer, however you want to say it."

She takes another step closer.

"I'm sorry for making you feel like you had to keep something from me and for not listening when you wanted to explain, which completely validates why you wanted to keep that secret in the first place." She nibbles on her bottom lip, driving me crazy. "I'm sorry for being so jealous of Angela." Chrissy glances over at Angela, who is dancing with a knight. "She's really very sweet now that I've spent some time with her."

And we have entered the Twilight Zone. "I should have told you she was on board."

She holds out a hand to stop me from saying anything else as she comes to a stop right in front of me. "You have a good heart. No more secrets, okay?"

"None." My heart leaps inside my chest because if she gives me the chance, I will prove that I am totally devoted to her, every single day for the rest of my life.

After she takes a deep breath, she takes me by the hands and says, "I'm sorry for not saying yes when you proposed. I was scared and I didn't want to mess things up, but I did anyway. That's my superpower."

I scrub my face with my hands. "I shouldn't have jumped to conclusions about why you didn't accept. All I had to do was ask you, but I have a tiny bit of a confidence problem, if you haven't noticed."

"Ya think?" Her sassy wink has me grinning from ear to ear.

I love how she's able to lighten the mood with one simple statement.

"Anyway..." She peeks around me, and I follow her gaze to where Angela and Charmaine are standing. Angela gives her a thumbs-up. *Weird.*

This is all so totally confusing, and I shake my head. "What's going on?"

Chrissy licks her lips, throws her head back, then drops to one knee. Gasps can be heard around us, as well as a few *awws*.

"Deacon Michael Youngblood, otherwise known as Grishork, the Sea Demon. The other day, you asked me when I thought I would be ready to get married again, and I said I didn't know. But I do know now. I am completely ready. I love you with all my heart, and I want to spend the rest of my life with you. Will you marry me?" She holds out the friendship ring for me to take.

All eyes are on me as everyone waits for my answer with bated breath. I stare at the prince, who taps his fake sword as though if I don't say something soon, he might put me in jail with Elliot. I glance over at Angela, who gives me a nod. I glance at Elliot, who slumps his shoulders but then throws his hands up in surrender, like he's admitting defeat.

Chrissy clears her throat from the deck where she remains kneeling. She cocks up an eyebrow with an "I'm waiting" expression.

As I crouch down next to her, a tiny gasp comes out of her mouth while her eyes get big with anticipation.

I whisper in her ear, "As long as the rest of our lives begins today, then my answer is absolutely yes."

She throws her arms around my neck, and I pick her up to swing her around. To the crowd, she yells, "He said yes!"

LARP music lilts through the air as the players dance around us. I plant a quick kiss on Chrissy's lips then pull back to rest my forehead on hers. "Will you wear that wench costume on our wedding day?"

With a twinkle in her eye, she replies, "As long as you wear what you have on too. You are the sexiest sea demon I've ever seen."

"And you've seen a few?"

Chrissy taps her chin as she mulls over my words, then replies, "Enough to know you're the one for me."

She slips the friendship ring onto my pinkie, and I stare at it and all that it represents. I may never take it off. I hug her so hard that she may not be able to breathe. I've never been so happy in all my life, and I can't wait to get off this ship and get married to this wonderful, free-spirited, beautiful gem.

She points in the direction of the fake jail, and I follow her gaze. With a snort, she says, "I didn't see that coming."

Monique opens the jail door and slips in with Elliot to give him a hug and a quick peck on the cheek. I quirk up an eyebrow and catch Chrissy doing the same. She *woo-hoo*s the jailed couple then stares up at me. "Courage. Wisdom. Power."

Without even having to think about it, I reply with the only phrase that fits my current mood. "Lightning bolt!"

Epilogue

Chrissy

It's hard to believe that only three months ago, Deacon and I were so close to never reconciling, but here we are now, only minutes away from getting married. A faint breeze blows through the tent that we girls are using as a staging room at Elmington Park. It's only fitting that we get married here because I wanted all our new friends in Nashville's premiere LARPing group to attend. It's practically sacred ground for us now, where we spend every Sunday afternoon learning how to parlour and improving our back story. Something is magical about this group of people.

Celtic music wafts through the air as April, Bailey, and Claire fuss over me to make sure my wedding dress and makeup are perfect. As much as I wanted to get married in my wench costume, I decided to shake it up a bit and wear something more appropriate for the occasion: a lavender midi dress with faint butterflies embroidered on the tulle overlay. The corset top is cinched in the back, and the best part is that it has pockets. Angela said it was perfect. We text almost every day, and she's bummed she can't attend the wedding. She's currently in the Bahamas as the *Sovereign of the Seas'* fitness director, living her best, sober life.

Behind me, a male clears his throat, and I turn to see my father standing there, beaming from ear to ear.

I turn in a circle, making the skirt swirl around me, showing off my bare feet. "Do you like it?"

Dad and I have come a long way in the last three months. When I stood up to him about not ever getting back with Elliot, saying I was in love with Deacon, he mellowed a lot. With some encouragement from Ty, he and Mom finally realized that I am my own person with unique views on life. They accepted Deacon like he's always been part of the family, and Dad has even accepted that I do not want to work for him. To really shock me to the core, he put me in touch with one of his clients, the CEO of Southern Hearts Greeting Cards. Along with my fortune-writing business, I am now a freelance greeting card writer. SHGC loved my Hearts of Fortune pitch, and I'm excited about this new venture.

It didn't take long for Elliot to get over me because, apparently, he and Savannah Von Locke are madly in love. With her family background, she definitely suits what he's looking for in a life partner. We all went to school together, and now that I think about it, she's always tried to get his attention, but he was too hung up on me to see what was right in front of him. I hope they make each other happy.

Dad's misty-eyed expression is something I don't see very often, but I love that he's showing more of his human side these days. He even sought out Deacon's advice on a golf injury a few weeks ago, something I *never* thought would happen.

"You are so beautiful. Deacon is one *fortune*-ate guy."

My dad made a pun? What is this world coming to?

April sprays a renegade hair on my head and says, "It's time."

She rushes out of the tent, along with Claire and Bailey, to the sound of a violin playing "I Can't Help Falling in Love with You," a song that pays homage to my parents' wedding but with a Celtic twist to the arrangement.

Dad takes my hand as we exit the tent toward our guests in the park. Some sit on blankets, while others have brought lounge chairs. I set up special seating for our parents because I didn't think they were thoroughly on board with lying back as though they were at a picnic. It's the least I could do since we chose not to do a traditional church wedding.

While April, Claire, and Bailey stand at the gazebo entrance opposite Drake, Aaron, and Ty, I get my first glance at Grishork, my sea demon. Deacon is wearing his costume from our cruise, and I have to grip my father's hand to stay upright because he is so stunning that my knees grow weak. He's absolutely the most beautiful man I've ever seen. But nothing is like the expression on his face when he turns to see me. He cups his hands to his face and swipes a tear from his eye. His brother Drake, the best man, pats him on the back in support.

I know the walk is only about thirty seconds at the most, but it feels like an eternity until we make it to the gazebo. Deacon takes my hand to walk up the steps where our officiant, Charmaine, waits to marry us. When I told her we were getting married, she took it upon herself to become a licensed marriage officiant. Since her business has a satellite office in Tennessee, she was able to become a notary to legally marry us. Leave it to her to find a way.

I don't remember anything that Charmaine says, but something made everyone in the audience laugh, which makes me blink my way out of my Deacon-induced haze. The only thing I can focus on is my husband. He's so handsome that it hurts to look at him, but that doesn't stop me from gazing into his beautiful eyes as he and I say, "I do." He tugs me close and wraps his arms around me. I slide my hands up his chest as we kiss for the first time as a married couple.

He grins against my lips. "We did it."

After an additional peck, I wink. "We sure did. Grishork, you are one sexy sea demon."

Deacon chuckles as he grasps my hand and kisses each knuckle. "Ready to start this adventure together?"

There is nothing in this world I would rather do. "Absolutely."

In a bellowing voice, Charmaine says, "Ladies and gentlemen of this world and of the land of Dur Demarion, it is my pleasure to introduce you to Mr. and Mrs. Youngblood."

The crowd claps, and the LARPers raise their foam swords in the air in celebration as we walk back through the park arm in arm. There is nothing I wouldn't do for this amazing man. I'll dress up in a duck costume or even go on another cruise with him as long as the theme is "clothing optional."

Acknowledgments

To Jymie and Kelly: You two are the only ones I trust with my terrible first drafts. I love both of you so much.

To Erica, Diane, Kelly, and Lynn at Red Adept Publishing: I appreciate all your help, guidance, and belief in me.

To Mark and Maddie: You are my entire world.

To Zacchaeus, Lydia, Daisy, Mae, and Jethro: I love that all my sweet fur babies were alive at some point during the evolution of this project. I'll never forget you all.

About the Author

After several decades of writing medical research documents, Cindy Dorminy decided to switch gears and become an author. She wanted to write stories where the chances of happy endings are 100% and the side effects include satisfied sighs, permanent smiles, and a chuckle or two.

Cindy was born in Texas and raised in Georgia. She enjoys gardening, reading, and bodybuilding. She can often be overheard quoting lines from her favorite movies. But her favorite pastime is spending time with Mark, her bass-playing husband, and Maddie Rose, the coolest girl on the planet. She also loves her fur child, Daisy Mae. She currently resides in Nashville, TN, where live music can be heard everywhere, even at the grocery store.

Read more at www.cindydwrites.com.

About the Publisher

Dear Reader,

We hope you enjoyed this book. Please consider leaving a review on your favorite book site.

Visit https://RedAdeptPublishing.com to see our entire catalogue.

Check out our app for short stories, articles, and interviews. You'll also be notified of future releases and special sales.